GUARDED MOMENTS

GUARDED MOMENTS

William J. Sunke

iUniverse, Inc.
New York Lincoln Shanghai

GUARDED MOMENTS

iUniverse books may be ordered through booksellers or by contacting:

iUniverse
2021 Pine Lake Road, Suite 100
Lincoln, NE 68512
www.iuniverse.com
1-800-Authors (1-800-288-4677)

Author Photo by: Jay Riggler

Cover Graphic by: Jafar Ghafarpour

ISBN-13: 978-0-595-41557-1 (pbk)
ISBN-13: 978-0-595-85904-7 (ebk)
ISBN-10: 0-595-41557-1 (pbk)
ISBN-10: 0-595-85904-6 (ebk)

Printed in the United States of America

To
my wife
for helping me to break
through the walls of my life,
especially the hardest,
myself

No two men differ as much as one man does from his former self.

—Pascal

Contents

Prologue

A large part of my life I've spent inside walls—some visible, others not. Over nine of those years I was a correctional officer at San Quentin Prison.

As a graduate of the first class of the Correctional Officers Academy, created to replace on-the-job trained, often brutal, guards with professional, compassionate correctional officers, I've walked the tiers of Death Row. And worked in the more dangerous Adjustment Center not long after three guards and three inmates were murdered, their throats cut by fingernail clippers.

During my career as a Correctional Office I've been stabbed and shot, yet I've had my life saved, minutes before it would have ended, by an inmate risking his own life to warn me. I've seen acts of unspeakable cruelty yet also witnessed acts of humbling kindness.

All those years I kept a secret I've never shared until now. Each day when I crossed the yard, I knew I could have been wearing another uniform—the blue of the inmates, not the green of the correctional officers.

Without exaggeration, I can state that had events taken a different turn in my youth, I would have arrived earlier at San Quentin as a prisoner, continuing the legacy of my grandfather, father, and brother, all three of whom served sentences inside the same walls.

To honor the lost time of three generations of Woolf, and to offer hope that the fourth, my son, may have his future beyond walls, I decided to tell my story.

If I can help one reader to find the Amy in his life or to heed a stranger offering life-changing advice, or to realize life-transforming change is always near, no matter how lost one feels, no matter how dark things appear, my journey back inside the walls will not be in vain.

Follow me then. I know the way by heart.

-#-

1

Terror in a Child's Eyes

Easter morning I received a phone call from the office at San Quentin, asking if I wanted an easy overtime day. I decided to take it, and the lieutenant told me that I would be working the Visiting Room.

In that area of the prison, correctional officers are in direct view of the public. It's not the same as being behind the walls, dealing with inmates on a one-on-one basis. I had to interact with the inmates and their families. There's a different mind-set there. Many of the correctional officers who worked the Visiting Room considered inmates' families future employment, thinking the kids would grow up to be like their fathers and they'd end up at San Quentin. Me? I didn't have such cynicism or fatalism. I don't believe a child has to repeat the wrongs of his father.

On this particular day, I saw a little boy who brought back all the stress and emotions I felt with my mother while going to visit my father behind bars.

I didn't want to go through it again, but found myself reliving the experience. Watching the boy and his family in the Visiting Room, I recalled that all I wanted to do was run outside and hide in my mother's car. But I couldn't leave the prison. I had to wait, just as I would have to wait again—as a correctional officer this time. That Easter morning while I worked the Visiting Room, two incidents occurred. To me, they conveyed the range of behavior that can occur behind the walls. In its own way, each incident showed why I always needed to be relaxed and alert at the same time.

There's a process for getting into the Visiting Room. Family members park in the main visitor lot, walk up the stairs, and enter the first coordination center. Visitors' names have to be posted on a list. After identification is verified, families go on to a second room where they are searched. Anything they bring in has to be checked, everything from purses to diaper bags.

The staff even check the milk in bottles to make sure nothing illegal is coming in. Basically, they are looking for any kind of contraband that can be smuggled in by a wife or family member of an inmate.

While they are going through this process, correctional officers are questioning everyone, even children. Families are requested to remove their shoes before passing through an X-ray machine. It's nerve-racking for visitors, especially people visiting San Quentin for the first time.

Once they are cleared, families have a quarter-of-a-mile walk to reach Visiting Gate Number Two, which provides access to the main prison grounds.

They're still not in the prison itself, but here identification is checked again. An officer may spot-check a purse, or might ask children if "mommy" asked them to hold anything to bring in. They'll inspect photos, lipstick tubes, envelopes—in fact, absolutely anything that can be carried in.

From there, visitors enter one of the main corridors leading from the walkway into the prison itself. When they glance up, they'll see massive walls towering above them, and men with rifles watching.

Kids start to get a sense that it's a different world than the one they know. Children start getting nervous at this point. They don't know what to think. All that they understand is that their father has gone away, and this is where he's gone.

Once they've passed through the next gate, they'll make a left and continue toward the Visiting Room. Relatives need to follow a specific pathway. They must stay inside the yellow lines. If they step outside those yellow lines or let their children wander past them, their visit will be cancelled. Visitors are no longer allowed to do what they want to do. Inside the walls, people do exactly what they're told.

Once family members are passed through into the actual visiting room, they'll be assigned to a specific table.

They go sit at that table and no other. While waiting, sometimes only for a few minutes, sometimes for half an hour, inmates will be undergoing searches. Their clothing will be checked and their body orifices examined to make certain they have hidden nothing to pass on to visitors. Within minutes, forty or fifty more inmates in blue denim shirts and Levis, will emerge from a back door—one by one, like from an assembly line.

Inmates may sit with family members, but they are not allowed to have any physical contact. Kids, though, can't be prevented from hugging their fathers.

That Easter morning, visiting had already been underway for over an hour. I was relaxed and joking with colleagues. Correctional officers don't expect anything to happen in the Visiting Room. Monitoring the area makes up for some of the other overtime jobs that aren't so pleasant.

I was moving around the room, making sure that everything was going smoothly. While greeting some of the families I had seen before, I paused to scan the faces. I could tell who'd been there many times and who was there for the first time. The newcomers were the ones I had to keep a close eye on, reminding them of the rules.

In walked a lady with a little boy who couldn't have been more than six or seven. I could tell by the way she was fumbling with her bag that this was her first time at San Quentin. I never did find out why her husband got put away. It doesn't matter. What matters is when I saw the frightened expression of the little boy, I couldn't take my eyes off him. The mother was struggling to close her purse while her son gripped her side.

Although I had seen a lot of children visiting their fathers, and most looked frightened, there was something different about the boy, almost familiar, as though, strangely, I understood his fear. I could tell he didn't understand what was going on. He was scared because he didn't know why his father was in prison or why uniformed men were watching his mother and him in the Visiting Room.

All around, he had correctional officers telling his mother what to do, where to go, and where to sit, and warning him that if he misbehaved he and his mother would be escorted out without a second warning.

As the officers continued giving the little boy orders, I watched him grow more frightened. "That's no way to talk to a six or seven year old," I thought. The boy was already terrified, and the more he was told, the more anxious and stressed he appeared.

I stood across the room, watching him clutch his mother then sit down with her across the room.

Shortly, the father came through the other door. Seeing him, the boy gaped. He didn't know what to do or what to say to his own father.

Watching them, I could hardly move. "What's going on?" I asked myself, then realized that little boy was me—when I was seven-years-old going to visit my father for the first time in prison—and scared to death of what was going to happen next. Were they going to let me back out? Did I have to stay there? Who were all the huge men with shaved skulls and tattooed arms, some with faces scarred by fights and stabbings?

I found myself drawn toward the boy, watching him pull his chair closer to his mother. She leaned over and began whispering to him. I sensed she was trying to reassure him everything was going to be okay.

As I passed, I heard her say, "We're here to see your father. Be a big boy. Don't cry."

The words echoed through me: "Be a big boy. Don't cry." They were the same words my mother had said: "Don't cry."

How do you not cry when you're terrorized by where you are and feel overwhelming helplessness?

When the inmate sat down at the table, the little boy didn't know if he should give his father a hug or even talk to him. The boy could only sit motionless, staring at him.

I couldn't help watching the exchange. Then one of the other officers came up, nudging me: "Woolf … Woolf, where are you? You're supposed to be paying attention to what's going on."

"I'm looking at that little kid over there," I said, smiling at the little boy now looking in my direction. His face was blank—as though he was uncertain how to respond. If he smiled, maybe he would get in trouble.

I made a slight wave with my hand.

The boy smiled a little—just enough for me to know it was a smile.

"I want my daddy back," he said.

"I know. He'll be home soon," I said.

The mother and father paused in their conversation—not sure if they should silence their child.

I bent down so that only the boy and his parents could hear me. "You know your dad is good. Not everybody here's a bad person. They've made a mistake and they must come here. It's like being restricted at home when you're sent to your room, except here, it's a big room and you have to stay inside longer."

The boy stared at me for a moment, then nodded.

The mother looked up at me. "Thank you, mister." she said softly.

The inmate glanced up. "Thanks, Woolf."

"It's okay," I replied, remembering sitting near far from where that the boy was when I was his age, watching everything that was going on around me. But no guard had tried to make me feel better.

I started away from the table.

The correctional officer who criticized me for not paying attention came over. "What are you doing talking with that kid?" he asked

"Look at him. He's scared to death," I answered.

"Forget him," the officer replied. "His dad's an inmate, Woolf. You shouldn't be too nice to these kids. They're going to be back one day to do their own time."

I looked the officer in the eyes. "Who do you think you are?" I said, trying to keep my voice down. "That's just a child. He doesn't know what's going on. All he sees is guns and guards and tough-looking men who could crush him in an instant. Most of all, he doesn't know why his father's here."

"Why do you care all of a sudden, Woolf?"

"Because I do. I don't want to work with you again if that's the attitude you have about kids coming to the Visiting Room with their mothers. It's not just the boy. It's the attitude you showed to his father. I have to walk next to his cell all day. I can get killed because you've got that messed-up attitude."

That moment was disturbing. In prison, once a correctional officer, or C.O., makes a statement defending an inmate, other officers start talking.

Sure enough, before visiting hours were over, another officer muttered, "You're soft, Woolf."

"No, I'm not," I replied. "You just have no idea what that kid's feeling."

"How the hell do you know what he's feeling?" he snapped.

It would have been a waste of time to explain to that C.O. how I knew what that kid was going through: the anxiety, the fear, the stress.

"Be a man." I remember my mother saying that as we waited for my father. "Your father loves you. It's important we be strong when he sees us."

I realized what I hadn't before. My mother had been focused on visiting her husband—just as this mother before me was. But neither my mother nor this boy's mother were aware of how much stress their sons were being put through.

More than anything, I wanted to make certain that little boy was protected from anything that would leave a scar in his memory, even though I sensed that the Visiting Room had already been branded inside him. There was no way to make the prison less threatening than it was. I could only hope to prevent it from becoming worse.

Seeing the daughters, sons, wives, and relatives coming in to visit with family members just to have a little time together, I felt the enormous weight of their combined fear.

I glanced around the room and then looked down at my correctional officer's uniform. "How did I get inside this place?" I wondered. It was a question I had never allowed myself to ask; now that I had, I couldn't stop thinking about it.

As I moved through the room, I kept glancing back at the little boy and sensing I had become part of the same world that had terrified me when I came to visit my father in prison. It was like I was serving a prison sentence, one no judge had meted out—but one which I had given myself: life behind bars.

Why was I here, in uniform, watching over inmates and their families, in a maximum security prison? What crime known only to me had I committed to sentence myself behind bars?

That day in the Visiting Room was different. Before, whenever I finished a shift, I knew I could go home—leave the walls behind me. But this day was unlike any other.

Seeing the terrified boy was like having a jagged mirror thrust up in front of me—holding up not only a painful reflection but opening a deep hole I found myself falling inside.

-#-

2

Big Bad Woolf

When I gaze back at my childhood and ask, "Where did everything start to go wrong?" I cannot point to a precise moment or incident that altered the direction of my life. I can only make out a subtle but unmistakable change settling over everything—the way daylight fades before the approach of night.

We were living in Pacifica, California then: my mother and father, my sister Gina, and my brother Griff. At seven, I was the eldest, followed by Gina, a year younger, and Griff, three years my junior.

From the outside, we resembled a typical white middle-class family living in a suburb of San Francisco during the 1960s. Both my parents worked days and would leave us in the care of a babysitter. My father was gone a lot, not only nights but weekends, too. He kept his business to himself, but my mother said he worked for a food company. Every once in a while he would return with boxes of candy and gifts for us. There were no police around then. Everything seemed quiet on the surface, filled with a strange stillness, like before a typhoon.

Change, when it came, started with my father's temper. Gina, Griff, and I could usually tell when it was building up, and we would take steps to stay out of his way. We weren't always successful. We got hit, but so did a lot of kids in those days. But my father's anger seemed to grow more explosive, and erupt more often. The back of his hand gave way to belts and straps. I don't know if it was a result of the whippings, but my schoolwork began to deteriorate and I frequently ended up in the principal's office.

About that time, I started noticing my father bringing home more and more people. There were loud and drank a lot. I didn't understand what alcohol could do then—but I could see that when my father drank for a while, he would change. Whatever patience he had evaporated, and his temper, hovering an instant away, would flash forward.

One afternoon we were playing darts in the backyard, and Gina had dared Griff to try to hit her. He did, the dart glancing off her head. She ran crying into the house. Moments later, my father had Griff and me lined up against a wall in the kitchen. He began throwing darts at us, yelling for us to keep our hands at our sides every time we raised them to cover our faces. My mother finally got him to stop.

My mother was a buffer against his outbursts—coming between my father and Griff, Gina, or me as he prepared to bring his belt down. Griff, though, was singled out for more punishment—not because of any particular thing he had done, but because he was failing at school. It was like all the stress at home was sinking into Griff and slowing him down, turning off all the things that make a boy grow inside. The change in Griff seemed to grow stronger, as though he was having a harder and harder time grasping the simplest things. He was becoming different, almost detached. I could feel my brother fading away, almost disappearing as he stood beside me while we were both hit by our father.

Once Griff and I found several cans of paint and decided to have a paint fight. While we were in the basement, two men in suits knocked on the front door and said they were looking for my father. I said he wasn't home. Since they seemed to be friends of my father, I said I thought he would be returning in a few minutes, and I let them in. As I went back to the basement, they asked if they could come down for a look. I didn't see anything wrong with letting them.

When they came downstairs, they started snooping around. Within minutes, they found a stack of license plates and immediately left. Later, I learned my father had been arrested and my grandfather had to bail him out of San Francisco city jail.

Fortunately, Griff and I didn't get punished for letting the plainclothes policemen into the house. But it was then that I first learned that my father was breaking the law.

I wasn't the only one who knew. Kids in the neighborhood started to say things about my father and the people he associated with—things that I didn't want to believe were true. I didn't know it at the time, but my father's name began appearing in the newspaper; as a result, the neighbors saw his name and told their children not to play with us.

Kids began shying away from us after school. It was as though Gina, Griff, and I had some disease everyone was afraid to catch.

Then teachers started treating us differently from the way they treated the other students. It didn't help that after the principal gave Griff a spanking, my father went up to school and threatened to beat him up if he ever touched one of us again.

Then, to make sure that Gina, Griff, and I got good grades, my father started going out with one of our female teachers. His actions only increased the rumors and worsened his reputation.

Whenever I would hear people say something bad about my dad, it was as though they were talking about me. My name was the same as his, even down to the middle initial. And my grandfather was named Rudy J. Woolf as well. It wasn't fair, I thought, the three of us having the same name. I used to imagine my grandfather, my father, and me stacked on top of each other, like some crazy totem pole. And I couldn't get out from under the bottom. I would just have to live out my name ... the name of my father ... the name of his father.

"What's in a name?" I asked myself. Everything and nothing, I came to realize.

My father must have sensed he wasn't spending much time with us, so to show he could be a dad like the other boys, he became a Cub Scout leader. In fact, he was so motivated that he became head of five Scout packs. Because of his business skills, he was soon put in charge of the Cub Scout bank account.

A few weeks later, there was a big meeting of the Cub Scouts in the school auditorium. Everyone was present. My father was supposed to be on stage with the other pack leaders. But he didn't show up.

Within days, I heard that my father had gone to the bank and withdrawn all the Cub Scout money—then spent it on a spree in San Francisco. Later, he was ordered to give back some of the money, but it was too late. The damage had been done. I was Rudy J. Woolf's son: Rudy J. Woolf. Needless to say, my career as a Cub Scout was short-lived.

People not caught up in the net of my father's deals saw only a charming, charismatic figure. Women were drawn to him. When he walked into a room, a spotlight seemed to materialize out of nowhere to focus on him. He was over six feet tall and wiry, with wavy blond hair, penetrating blue eyes, and an easy smile. Of German descent, not Sicilian or Italian, my father wasn't a "made man," but he was "connected" like other young guys coming up in the mob.

Even though I could tell that people respected him, I could see they were also afraid of my father. For myself, I felt safer when he would go away on one of his trips.

Yet whenever he returned, he would be irritable. Whatever patience he had had eroded. He grumbled about the children. If we did anything wrong, he immediately spanked us.

He used to play a little game in the kitchen when my mother would prepare dinner. He would make Gina, Griff, and me line up against the wall.

"Who do you love the most?" he would ask us.

My mother would tell him to stop, but he would ignore her.

There was no secret. Gina, Griff, and I knew we would have to say, "You," or get knocked down.

Basically, he was checking. It was his own private loyalty test. He wanted to make sure that we loved him more than we did my mother.

Even though my mother knew we were trapped into giving our answer, I could see that she was hurt. If one of us had dared to answer, "Mom," it would have been terrible for us. So every time our father made us play his savage game, we answered "You."

"See, Lucille," he'd say to my mother. "They love me more than they love you."

My mother would only nod. Thank God for my mom. As long as she was there, my father couldn't go straight at us. His anger was deflected by her presence. She was a buffer against all that was cruel and mean in him. I don't know how she did it—veer him away from us, soften him when he would be in a drunken rage, but she saved us time and time again.

During one of my father's absences he was serving time at an honor farm in Northern California. My mother would take us to visit him. It was during those visits to my father behind bars or barbed wire fences that I first felt the terror I later saw in the eyes of the little boy at San Quentin.

Our neighbors soon learned my father was back in jail. As Gina, Griff, and I would walk to school, faces would turn away and voices would drop as we passed. It was as though we had been exiled to an island no larger than ourselves for something we had not done.

When my father was released, he went back into business—apparently more successfully than ever, for we soon moved into an upscale neighborhood in Mill Valley. Griff, Gina, and I were happy to leave our old school behind and start new, free of the rumors and gossip about our father.

The pace of life in Marin County seemed faster, as though by leaving Pacifica things would never go slowly again. Everything started taking place at a speed too fast for us to control or understand ... until much later.

It didn't take long for the novelty of moving into a new home to end. My parents started arguing more frequently and more harshly.

I tried to drown out their shouting voices—not by putting my hands over my ears, but by withdrawing. I tried to pull away from people, creating a sort of wall between my father and me. I didn't know if it was the same kind of wall Griff had gone behind or the one Gina was concealed behind. I sensed that each of us was trying as much as possible to be invisible to our father.

He wasn't always in a bad mood. One New Year's Eve he had a big party, and I remember coming downstairs in the morning, stepping over the sleeping and passed-out guests from the night before. Bodies were everywhere—sprawled on sofas, chairs, even on the floor. Later that same day, my father had a barbecue. Everybody had a great time. My father had an excitement about him that seemed to animate everything he said. To me, it was as though his personality was like a magic wand: One end was rainbow colored, able to hypnotize strangers and friends; the other end was dark and used to hit us.

Within a year, we moved again, this time to San Anselmo. My father was gone more and more frequently. I started to have a difficult time at school. I had problems with spelling, mathematics, and with staying up with the rest of my classmates. I developed a fear of leaving the house. Gina, too, started experiencing the same fear. Again, our father's reputation had preceded us and had transformed what could have been friendly encounters into uncomfortable moments where it felt like we had already been judged.

I felt sad all the time, but because I didn't know it, I just thought the world was the same way I felt.

The teachers took note of my failing grades and poor attendance. I was tested, and I failed most of the tests. Back then, time wasn't spent looking into a student's home-life to explain his poor performance. I was simply classified as a slow-learner. I think I just wanted to be near my mother, and by not trying at school I thought I would get to spend more time with her. My mother worked with me, trying to motivate me and to help me raise my grades. But I could feel gears locking inside me. It was like an enormous machine called I CARE ABOUT SCHOOL was grinding to a stop.

The final blow was that I was held back that year. Of course, my father said there was nothing wrong with me. How could there be? I was his namesake.

Again, like a solution for everything that was wrong with our family, he moved us. There was never an explanation. He would merely tell us, "We're getting out of here."

After only eight months in Mill Valley, we moved to another area of Marin. Strangely, things seemed to calm down in Larkspur. I don't know if my father was making a lot of money, but he appeared be in a better mood. This calm quickly translated to the children. There was now a fourth, Kelly, who was five years younger than me.

To tell the truth, maybe things felt more stable because I was older. Even though I was still a kid and didn't understand my father any better than I ever did, I did feel that I was better able to ride out his storms. I knew how to tell in an instant, from the moment he walked in the door, what mood he was in. I got better at being able to look out the upstairs window before he would even appear, feeling in the darkness my father moving toward the house, and gauging in his footsteps, in the way his hands hung at his side, whether he was drunk or sober, whether the sea inside him was stormy or calm. My judgment was seldom wrong.

I took his advice, "Watch what is going on around you," but came to realize he should have added, "Most of all—watch me." I had to learn that part on my own.

My father started to take me around with him in San Francisco, stopping at one business after another. I never saw so much cash go back and forth. It seemed like a blur of green, whisking from one hand to another, out of one paper bag into another, while I stood by, ignorant of everything I was witnessing. But of one thing I was certain: My father was good at what he did. Whenever he would pull up in front of a bar or restaurant, he always told me, "Keep your ass right in that seat." Then he would go inside the club and return a few minutes later carrying a brown paper bag stuffed with money.

Whenever I asked about the people we met, he would always say, "Keep your mouth shut and watch what's going on around you." I took his words to heart, most of all when it came to him. I watched his every move, for I could never tell whether a smile would come next ... or a fist.

With him on those nights in San Francisco, I grew to feel I had been adopted into a new family—but to stay a member, I had to earn their respect and their trust. I had to be an "earner" and to keep my mouth shut.

I had never seen my father's charm fail to work, hour after hour, day in, day out. Never once did he lose his temper as he had with us at home. Never once did his smile break. He was always impeccably dressed in expensive suits, and he always seemed to know the most important person wherever we went. Everyone knew him, too. Handshake after handshake, pat on the back after pat on the back, free drinks, and a Roy Rogers, a non-alcoholic drink, for me. I felt as though I was basking in the halo of a famous person, a father I didn't know.

Then he would suddenly disappear—and it would come out that he was in jail. Nothing more would be said until he walked back in the door, carrying gifts or nothing at all, as though he were merely a salesman back from a long trip. I don't know what Gina or Griff felt then—our little sister luckily was too young to know, but I began acting as though it were the most natural thing to have a father who went in and out of jail.

Back the family went behind barbed wire fences, back behind more walls, and past more guards to visit him. Every time we protested about going to see him, our mother would silence us. "He wants to see all of you," she would tell Gina, Griff, and me. She even brought along the youngest, Kelly, clutching her in her arms the way I would later see another mother carry a baby inside prison walls.

Things changed after he was released the next time. Police started coming to the house to ask him about his whereabouts, or if he knew about something I could never really hear, for they would be talking in whispers, trying to prevent the children from hearing what was going on. I got good at watching the police, almost able to read their lips when they asked my father where he had been the night before.

Everything changed with a phone call my mother got. I don't know what was said but she got a look of fear in her eyes I'd never seen before—even when my father was at his worst. She was scared. Hanging up, she immediately called him and said that a man had just called, saying that my father had cheated him on an automobile deal; if things weren't made right, he was going to come over to Marin and kill her and all the children.

I didn't really know what was going on, except that my father called back a little later and told my mother to keep all the kids in the house while he took care of things.

My father didn't come home that night.

As we opened the door to leave for school the next morning, there were three sheriff's cars in front and a sheriff's van in back. We went right back in the house.

What had happened came out quickly. My father knew who had threatened us and immediately drove to the man's apartment building in San Francisco. The man must have seen my father pull up for he took off across the roof, where my father caught up and shot him three times.

The bullets didn't kill him. Instead, the man fell off the roof, landing on the sidewalk, breaking both legs and an arm. The man never called our house again.

Afterward, my father walked downstairs, got into his car and drove away. A police officer followed him, making sure he made it safely across the Golden Gate Bridge, into Marin County, where he pulled up in front of our house, and found Marin County sheriffs waiting.

They took him to jail. Everything had happened so uneventfully that it seemed only natural that my father should be arrested one more time.

For a day reporters were outside the house, waiting to interview my mother when she came out. She knew not to say a word. So did we. The next day the reporters were gone and my mother thought it was safe for us to return to school.

In those days my school had a project called "Show and Tell," which required that students bring in an object from their homes or an item from the newspaper that they wanted to show to the class and tell them about. A friend of mine brought in the front page of the <u>Marin Independent Journal</u>. "Look," he said, holding up the article. "Woolf's father got arrested for shooting a guy in San Francisco."

The teacher immediately took the newspaper and sent the boy to the principal's office.

I was so ashamed I couldn't look at anyone.

Minutes later, I was called into the principal's office and told that I was being excused from school for the next two days.

That day destroyed any friendship Gina, Griff, and I had formed with other kids. If we were outsiders in Pacifica, we were now marooned.

The charge was soon dropped, and my father returned home. No explanation for what had happened. No questions about how we had fared with all the publicity. Silence reigned.

Some of the teachers weren't able to conceal their fear whenever my name was called: Rudy J. Woolf. To them, it was an echo from the name in the newspapers.

From that day on, school seemed hollow. I never went back to class to learn. I went there to wait for every class to end.

At home, my father was still playing his little game of having the children compete for his love.

There was a brief time when I wanted to learn to play the piano. So there was one week when we had a piano. Then my father got angry and the piano disappeared. So I tried drums. My mother bought me a drum set. Then he busted that up. Next, I wanted to learn to play the violin.

"That's sissy shit," he said, refusing to let me do it.

Christmas came and he was drinking and being nasty to my mother and us.

I don't know where the words came from, but I shouted, "Why don't you just go back to jail?"

I was knocked across the room.

My mother stepped in, protecting us, as she did again and again.

The next day, like a storm that had ended as quickly as it began, my father was in a great mood. There was no way of knowing what would come next. One could only survive by anticipating the worst. But the worst was beyond all my fears.

When I was almost twelve, my father was released from another work farm and began making fast money again. He wanted to move out of southern Marin to northern Marin.

We went to Bel Marin Keys in Novato, where we had a dock on the water. My father bought a boat; of course, Griff, Gina, and I became the crew.

My family had gotten larger. My mother had given birth to two more children, both girls: Doris, six years younger than I was, and Mandy, the youngest, seven years younger. Because of the age gap, they seemed separate from the world Griff, Gina, and I lived in with our father. It was as though the two youngest girls belonged to a different family. I was envious of how they had escaped so much that Gina, Griff, and I hadn't.

The spread in ages among the six children had a profound effect on how we were raised. Gina, Griff, and I were linked together, joined through every experience. The three younger girls, though—for Doris was more with the youngest two than with the three oldest—seemed unscathed, never at the business end of my father's anger. It was as though they were too young to be drafted into a war Gina, Griff, and I had already fought in, and would go on fighting until death, defeat, or victory put an end to our struggles.

At first, as with all our houses, everything at Bel Marin Keys seemed normal. We played with other children and explored the sand dunes. It was at the Keys that I developed my love of water. I enjoyed nothing more than jumping into the water, floating on my back, and looking up at the sky. Sometimes I would dive underwater and hold my breath as long as I could, for it was so quiet and calm below the surface.

It was a false calm, though, like the gifts our father would give us and then take to sell back when he was short of money. Every time he would give me a present, I felt like turning it around to see if there was a string wrapped around his hand and attached to the gift. I knew the string was there—even if it was invisible.

No matter how far away we moved from one house to another, my father's reputation followed him like an abandoned dog that always seemed to know where to find him.

I didn't know I was doing it at first—breaking the law. It didn't feel wrong, what I was doing: scaling the fence of an off-limits military place to crawl on my belly up to the flight line and watch cargo planes take off and land. "What harm was there in that?" I asked myself. "None at all," came the reply. Or eating a cheeseburger in a café and then running out without paying for it? Tiny infractions that hurt no one—like bugs splattering against the windshield of a speeding car. They didn't slow the car down, they didn't block the view ... at first.

At home, my father started taunting Griff and me about not being men unless we had been to jail. I don't know why but we started to buy into his tough-guy stuff. It didn't help that he pitted my brother against me to show who loved him more. It was an impossible contest to win and one we were both certain to lose. Only my father won, for he made the rules and then changed them for a new game.

The only thing I had come to count on from him was unpredictability.

Somehow through all the family troubles, Gina had managed to remain an excellent student. Griff, though, was getting worse grades than I had. My father used to taunt him, saying Griff had been born feet-first. His brain was deprived of oxygen and he would always be slow-minded as a result.

Griff absorbed all my father's taunts ... like a sponge unable to squeeze out what was true from what was false, what was good from what was toxic.

One day I came home from school and heard yelling even before I walked in the house. In the kitchen my mother was sprawled on the floor. Gina was cowering in the corner and Griff stood wincing as my father threatened him.

Abruptly, my father wheeled around and started to pull the china cabinet over on my mother. With only an instant to spare, she rolled out of the way of the shattering dishes and cups. I ran out to the garage and grabbed a baseball bat. Hurrying into the house, I held the bat up in front of my father. "You ever hit her again, I'll smash you with this."

He chased me out of the house. When he couldn't catch me, he got into his car and raced away. I went back into the house and helped clean up the mess in the kitchen.

Later, I learned that he went over to San Francisco and got drunk. On the drive back home, he rolled the car near Corte Madera. The station wagon burst into flames, but my father stumbled out safely and somehow made it home. He was so drunk, though, he forgot the two hundred thousand dollars he had collected in the city and had stuffed in a bag under the back seat.

The next day he got a phone call from the owner of a night club in North Beach who wanted to know where his money was. My father said it burned up in a car crash.

Two days later my mother received a basket of fruit from the Italian-American owner of the club. As for my father, he got a get-well card and a set of keys for a new car.

The destroyed money didn't matter. To the night club owner, it was more important that my father wasn't killed in the accident—because he had made money for the man in the past and would make more money in the future. He was part of a system that had its own form of unquestioning trust … as long as one remained loyal. The one unforgivable fault for my father and the people he worked for was disloyalty. Again and again, he lectured Griff, Gina, and me that loyalty was thicker than blood. We believed him, even if he was disloyal to us.

With our family, it was feast or famine. And at \Bel Marin Keys at that time, we seemed to have Christmas every day. My father was making big money, and he was trying to make up for all his violence by buying toys for the children.

He just kept bringing home more presents: dolls for the little girls, clothes for Gina, and hydroplanes for Griff and me. They were fast. Griff and I would race across the lagoon, swamping other kids in their slow canoes. We were the Woolf boys. If our father made big waves, we were going to make small ones. If people thought he was wild, we'd be wild, too.

Rumors started up again. This time, they were not about my father being arrested. This time, they concerned his affairs with married women in Bel Marin Keys. One afternoon a friend told me his father had forbidden him to see me again. "Why?" I asked, suspecting the answer would have something to do with my father. I was right. My friend's father had come home to find his wife and my father naked on the sofa. He ordered his wife to go upstairs and my father to leave.

My mother found out about his womanizing. She always knew he was unfaithful and would never change, but this time it had occurred in our neighborhood. I don't know who told her, but I could tell she was hurt. Soon her pain would stop.

Out of nowhere my father started saying he wanted to own horses. As though every impulse was meant to be obeyed, he bought a mare for Gina, then negotiated a deal for a horse that hadn't been ridden in a year. Although Mandy was too young to ride, my father said he wanted to take pictures of her and my mother on horseback.

Thanksgiving Day they went out to the stables. A groom saddled the horse my father had bought cheap, and my mother climbed up on the horse, with my father handing her the baby. Either the clicking camera or the baby's movements spooked the horse. It reared up and threw my mother, knocking her unconscious and fracturing her skull.

Instantly, my father returned to his car and took an M-1 rifle out of the trunk. Returning to where the horse was pacing near my mother, he emptied a clip of bullets into the animal. The police arrived before the ambulance did. Seeing the bullet-riddled horse on the ground, the officers asked my father what had happened. He said that after the accident, two hunters had passed by and, learning what the skittish horse had done, they shot it and left.

I was home and knew nothing of what had occurred. Gina, Griff, and I got off the bus, walked into the house, and found our aunt and grandmother waiting. My aunt said our mother had been in an accident and taken to the hospital. The baby had been brought back to the house by my father, but he wasn't there anymore. He was at the hospital and he called later, telling us our mother would be fine.

In the morning, I was the first one up and hurried down to find my grandmother in the kitchen. I asked what time my mother would be coming home. They didn't know, they said, but I wasn't to worry. She was fine and would be home in a couple of days. At that moment the door opened, and my father walked in with his brother and sister.

I don't think he saw me standing in the kitchen—even when he walked through the door and stopped by my grandmother. "Lucille's dead," my father said.

It's true what I had heard, that everything stops when something terrible happens.

I didn't cry. I kept waiting to cry, but no tears came. I was growing numb. I could sense a coldness moving through me. Even though I had no words for what I felt at that moment, I knew I was doomed. If I ever had a childhood, it ended then.

Moments later, my aunt told Gina what had happened. Then she tried to explain to my younger sisters the same news differently. I went upstairs to tell Griff. For a while, he kept telling me to stop kidding. Then he realized I was serious. He didn't cry either—at least not in front of me. He looked stunned, as though some enormous arrow had passed through him without leaving a hole, but had destroyed him in the process.

Much of what happened to Griff after our mother's accident was from knowing that he had lost his temper at our mother that morning and yelled at her that he wished she were dead. A day later she was.

My mother knew Griff didn't mean what he had said in anger, but Griff would forever carry inside him the guilt for what he'd said.

At my mother's funeral, Griff didn't want to go inside. Gina and Kelly were crying.

I stood beside the open casket, waiting for everyone to pass. Finally, when everyone had gone outside, I walked over and looked down at my mother's face. "What do I do now?" I thought. I stood waiting for her to open her eyes and answer my question, but she didn't. I knew then nothing would ever be the same.

-#-

3

Headless

Once my mother was gone, our house seemed to grow larger and emptier. My mother's presence had filled every room. Now her absence weighed on everything.

Doris and Mandy didn't understand where mother had gone. Gina, Griff, Kelly and I did, but couldn't explain what had happened. We could hardly tolerate the truth ourselves.

My aunt came and went, trying as best she could to take over the chores only a woman could do, and even if a man could have done them, my father would have refused. I came to understand what it meant to retreat into a bottle. For a while, he became less violent but drank more and more.

An argument must have occurred between my father and my aunt, for one day she stopped coming to help out.

I later learned that my father had convinced her to take out a loan to help save her house. Secretly, he made sure she couldn't repay the loan, then took possession of her home when she defaulted—after which he sold the house. My father had simply repeated what he had done after my grandfather died: taken out credit cards in his dead father's name and charged up thousands of dollars—debts that my grandmother had to pay off.

"Opportunist" would be the merciful way to describe him.

About then, my father became obsessed with having us clean the house. He kept having us scrub the toilets, the walls, the floors, and all with small brushes. When we had finished, he would inspect all the rooms; if he found we had missed a stain inside the tub or a scuff mark, we would have to start again. Sometimes he would wake us in the middle of the night and herd us downstairs to clean the kitchen floors.

Being the oldest, I started taking over cooking and cleaning, and taking care of my brother and sisters.

School was at the bottom of my list of priorities. I hadn't gone in weeks, and the attendance office had stopped calling to see where I was.

I felt I was no longer the same Rudy Woolf I was before my mother's death. I didn't know who I had become or what had happened to the boy I had been. One thing was certain: I had to take care of my family. If it meant cheating, I would cheat; if it meant stealing, I would steal. Whatever it took, I would do it to protect my family.

Women started to turn up at the house—not to care for the children, but to see my father. They came at night and left in the morning. I don't remember their names. I don't even think they told me.

One night, a neighbor's wife came over. She and my father had a few drinks and then went upstairs. They didn't close the door all the way, and when I went down the hall to my room I could see my father pulling the underpants off the woman, who was passed out on the bed.

Soon a woman named Nina appeared. She was a dancer, and my father had met her in San Francisco while my mother was alive. Nina had four daughters, and brought them with her when she came to spend the weekend with my father. Nina tried to be a mother to us—but my father done something to her, for after a few weeks she stopped coming. After Nina left, things seemed to settle in—like hardening cement. There would be my father and the six of us. No one could replace our mother and no woman would even try again. I could feel it in the way my father treated the different women. He wasn't interested in what they thought of us, or us of them. He only wanted the women for himself ... until he got bored or angry, and then they stopped coming back.

In California at this time, the Department of Motor Vehicles had a statute that a boy of thirteen, living on a ranch or farm, could be issued a driver's license. It was only good for operating farm equipment and could never be used at night.

My father got me a license. It didn't matter that we didn't live on a ranch or farm. Because his own license was suspended, he needed a chauffeur to take him from one bar to another, then back home. At thirteen, I found myself driving him through San Rafael at all hours of the night. Within a few weeks of becoming his chauffeur, I was being sent off alone on liquor runs. Before long, while he was sleeping late, I would go to get groceries for my siblings. A few months later he started having me take him into San Francisco. He liked to hit the bars and restaurants in North Beach. I'd sit in the car waiting, or if he was in a good mood, I could go inside and sit in the corner, quietly sipping a Roy Rogers.

One weekend, two of my uncles came to visit. After a while, they decided they wanted to go to North Beach, so my father had me drive them to the Peacock, a well-known club featuring topless dancers. Once inside, my uncles told my father that it was time for me "to lose my cherry." Laughing, my father called over a cocktail waitress he knew, and the next thing I knew she was talking to a single woman at the bar and pointing me out.

The woman came over and sat down. Even though she couldn't have been more than twenty-five or so, she seemed old. She was a grown woman taking my hand and saying we were going to go to her room. "Everything's been taken care of, honey," she whispered in my ear.

She lived in a dingy studio above another topless club. Just a room with a bed, a small bathroom, and a door-less closet full of clothes, mostly red.

After she chained the door, the woman started unbuttoning her blouse. She saw me hesitating. "Come on, sweetie, take off your clothes. I know it's your first time. I'm gonna make it so good you'll never forget it."

I unchained the door, hurried downstairs, and went back to the Peacock. When I told my father what the woman wanted me to do, he slapped me in front of everyone. "Get some balls! Get back up there and take care of business."

I went back and found the woman leaving her apartment. I told her I had changed my mind. She smiled and led me back upstairs. I got undressed and did as my father said and took care of business.

Maybe it was the freedom that the car offered or that my father was coming to depend on me more and more, but we started getting along better. My father began introducing me to all his friends. I was proud when he'd pat me on the shoulder. "This is my kid," he'd say.

At that time, the big hangout for anyone who was someone was the Blue Leopard Cocktail Lounge on Fillmore Street in the Marina District. Sitting at a booth with my father and his friends one night, I looked at a photograph behind the bar and noticed that it showed my father sitting with his arm around a young woman who was not my mother. I don't know why, but I felt surprised. I knew my father had been going out with other women before my mother died, but seeing the photograph in a crowded nightclub made it seem cruel to my mother's memory. Before, when my father would be gone for days, I would never really know what he was doing. My mother would always say he was out of town on business. Now I was actually with him.... "out of town" together.

A few weeks later my father got arrested for something and was going back to jail. He wanted me to take his place while he was gone. All I had to do, he said, was swing by a few places and pick up some paper bags. After I got them, I was supposed to take them to a man at Luca's Restaurant in North Beach. I'd even get paid. He said I'd make enough to buy a car or motorcycle. It sounded simple—taking paper bags from one person to another. Since I wasn't going to school, I was happy to do it. Like Griff, I just wanted to get my father's love and approval. Doing what he wanted was the best way I knew.

That's when I moved from accompanying my father to nightclubs to visiting them alone without him. I never realized how strange I must have looked, a fourteen-year old kid with a paper bag in his hand coming out of a topless bar or strip joint at night. But never once was I bothered. I'd simply go back where I had parked the car, open the trunk, put the bags inside, and go on to the next place. When I finished the last pickup, I would go to Luca's and always meet the same man, who would buy me whatever I wanted to drink, slip me a little wad of bills, and then take all the little bags out of the big bag with the slips of paper. I never once looked inside the bags. It wasn't my business; besides, I wasn't curious then.

After I had been dropping off the bags for a few weeks, the man opened them up and let me peek inside. They were filled with wads of ten and twenty dollar bills.

"How much is there?" I couldn't keep from asking.

"Sixty thousand or so," he replied.

I guess he figured I could be trusted, for I no longer went only to bars for the bag money. I started going to the best hotels, massage parlors, fancy restaurants. It would always be the same. I would only have to walk inside and look around before someone would come up to me with a paper bag. "Hey, Rudy, want a drink?"

"Sure, a Roy Rogers," I'd say, and I'd sit down for a few minutes before continuing my rounds.

When most people think of a bag, they see a kid at a supermarket loading groceries. I was a different kind of bag boy, and I think I was the youngest one in San Francisco then.

I always kept an eye out to make sure that I wasn't being followed. A fourteen-year-old kid carrying around bags of money was an easy target. That's when I started learning to read people and learning body language: how people made eye contact or avoided it. I learned to watch for bulges underneath a jacket and to recognize the look of straps on a shoulder holster under a coat. I started to see any stranger as a mystery I had to solve on the spot. My life depended on it.

After a few months, my father got released from jail and heard from his buddies that I had been doing a good job during his absence. It was hard for him to show gratitude. The most he could say was, "Your job is to make money, fuck as many women as you can, and stay out of jail."

I was waiting for my father to treat me better for what I had done for him. Not as an equal, I knew that couldn't be, but at least with respect. I was wrong. He never changed; I don't think he ever wanted to—or even thought about it. He was like a wall without a door. A door lets things in or out. My father wanted to keep everything sealed shut—like a prison.

My father decided to move again. He didn't tell us why but I suspected he had slept with so many married women in the neighborhood that it would only take one phone call to the police from an angry husband, saying the Woolf children were being left alone at night, for there to be a problem.

We left Bel Marin Keys and moved to an upscale neighborhood called Dominican Heights in San Rafael. Our new house was on the same street as that of the mayor and the chief of police—but we weren't the average family arriving. A single father with six children made an impression on the neighbors.

I kept right up with collecting money for my father. It made my father's job easier. But without telling him, I started my own business. I began setting up young women at different hotels and bars. I wasn't pimping, I reasoned; I was just introducing people and getting a commission for it—ten dollars from each girl for each encounter, and ten dollars from each hotel clerk for each time a room was used.

I remembered the warning my father had told me again and again: Keep your mouth shut and pay attention to what is going on around you.

Shy by nature, I kept quiet—but watched everything that went on. I made it a point to learn the names of all the club owners, the bartenders, the cocktail waitresses, even the bouncers; I tried to figure out the hierarchy of each business and the relationships among the different businesses themselves. It was like an enormous web extending over San Francisco, from hotel to bar, from taxi to waterfront café—and I wanted to know every filament of that web.

One night in North Beach I learned that my godfather had been arrested for selling a large amount of heroin to an undercover federal agent. My father said he was in big trouble—not because of the cops, but because my godfather had violated a fundamental rule not to deal drugs. Women, money, cars—my godfather had everything going for him, and he had risked it all to go off on his own.

A decision had to be made: Either kill him for breaking a cardinal rule or strip him of everything he owned. His associates waited to see what he would do when he went before the judge. The fact that he accepted the blame and didn't roll over on anyone saved his life.

I vowed then that I would never go to prison, and that I would have nothing to do with drugs.

For years, I broke both promises again and again.

My father and his friends made a little space for me in San Francisco. Although I wasn't simply seen as "Rudy's kid" any more, I still wasn't one of the guys. I had to go do the jobs no one else wanted.... like stealing license plates off cars sold to Chinese exchange students, who in those days weren't allowed to own private property, so they paid cash to be able to have the cars shipped back to China—and I'd steal the plates so they could be resold on different cars.

If there was a mirror then that would have given a reflection not of what I looked like, but who I was trying to resemble, I would have seen my father staring back. Even after all the terrible things he had done to my mother, my brother, my sisters, and me, I still couldn't help wanting to be ... like him. After all, we did have the same name. Not only was I making money, all in cash, but I started learning about multiple strings of income. To make big money, one job wouldn't do, and I had to get paid in cash to avoid paying taxes. All the money I earned, I kept hidden in a safe deposit box.

The thirteen-year-old boy I had been, driving alone into San Francisco the first night to pick up collection money, seemed like a friend I had dropped off long ago, to travel on alone.

My life was an enormous teeter-totter. I'd started drinking with my father and his buddies in North Beach—taking a sip of a Whiskey Sour here and a taste of someone's Gimlet there. Then I'd go home tipsy, only to be woken at four in the morning by my father, yelling for everyone to get downstairs and scrub and wax the kitchen floor.

Anything could set him off on a rampage, and we learned to run from him. Numerous times he would chase Gina, Griff, and me through the house. It would be hard on whomever he caught. Because he wasn't as quick as I was to see the blows coming, Griff started getting hit a lot more.

Watching Griff taking a pounding from my father, I swore that if I ever got married, I'd never hit my wife as he had my mother, or my children as he did us.

Why couldn't he just talk to us when we did something wrong? Why did he always have to hit us? I once asked my grandmother if my father had gotten hit by his father. She didn't reply—but the look on her face told me what I wanted to know. Fear and bribery were the constant emotional extremes of life with him. I used to imagine all of us being on an elevator either rising higher and higher—with a view overlooking everything—or else plunging out of control deeper into darkness. No place to get off in the middle. Our home was that elevator, and my father kept his hand on the controls. Either he was stalking us through the house or coming in the door with presents for everyone. No one could read him. Stop became Go. Love turned to Hate.

No wonder Griff started burglarizing houses. He wanted to show our father that he could be good at being bad. I wasn't going to be left behind. I started breaking into car dealerships and stealing parts. If someone wanted a set of magnesium rims, I'd get them. If some kid was owed money, I'd get the money for him.

I was heading in the same direction as the previous two generations of Rudy Woolfs. I was one arrest from going to juvenile hall; from there, prison was just ahead. Once things started falling, they just picked up speed.

When it came to choosing between staying in high school or earning money, I went for the money. I had a job at a pizza restaurant and because of what I'd learned in San Francisco, I started making money on the side. I'd sell beer to minors but at twice the price.

Growing up in Marin County, it was always anything-could-happen night. Whenever I got home, I didn't know if I'd find my father putting together a doll's house for Doris or Mandy, slapping a woman I'd never seen before, or having a party for thirty or forty people—half of whom were buddies from San Francisco, and the others judges and off-duty law enforcement officers from Marin Country.

I got to know some of the cops and asked one if I could accompany him on a ride-along.

The next Saturday night I was sitting beside him in a patrol car as we cruised through the shopping center at Strawberry in Mill Valley.

Suddenly, the dispatcher's voice came over the radio, giving an address and saying there were complaints of a loud party with guests firing automatic weapons across a field. The dispatcher gave an emergency code, requesting additional officers be sent to the address. It was our house.

The officer took the radio and confirmed the address.

"Yeah," snapped the dispatcher, "It's that crazy motherfucker Woolf. That son of a bitch. Man, we have more problems with him and his family. They should kick their asses out of Marin."

I was so stunned I couldn't speak.

The officer replied on the radio. "Hey, can we be a little bit more professional? I've got the young Woolf riding in the car with me."

The dispatcher came right back on the radio: "What, is he handcuffed in the backseat?"

"No, he's riding as an observer."

Woolf, Woolf, Woolf. The name was a chain I had to drag around with me everywhere I went; no matter how much I tried, I knew I could never break the links and free myself—because the links were made of flesh and blood.

A few nights later, my father started punching Griff and me. I stupidly went and got the shotgun in the garage. I wasn't thinking. I just shoved shells down both barrels, slammed it shut and ran back into the house.

My father stood in the kitchen, watching me take aim at him. "If you have any balls, go ahead, or you're going to suffer the consequences."

I couldn't "go ahead."

He could: The consequences were being hit hard enough to leave my imprint in the door. Even though he had hurt me once more, I was glad I hadn't fired. No matter how bad he was, I would have killed my own father, and who would have raised my sisters? I would have been found guilty of murder and condemned to death or at least to spend my life in prison.

I didn't want to end up on Death Row or serve a life sentence behind bars—but I didn't know how to stop my father from hurting me, or worse, how to stop myself from becoming more and more like him. I don't know what ostriches see when they stick their heads in the sand, but I can understand why they do it. They don't want to see a thing. That's how I became.

I wasn't the only one who felt trapped. Gina and Griff felt the same. We were going down hard and fast together, but totally alone in terms of the pain.

I was still picking up collection money in San Francisco, but now I was no longer considered a kid. Bar owners would shake my hand when I walked in and offer me free drinks and meals the way they did with my father and uncles. I was on my way to becoming one of them, another Woolf they could be proud of.

Then came what I call my last supper. To this day, I don't remember which North Beach restaurant it was in or how it began—but I was sitting at a table when a commotion broke out behind me.

"Fuck you," someone yelled.

Then a shot.

I turned to see the back of a man's head blown off.

I'm getting out of here, I thought. I knew I didn't have what it took to be as violent and vicious as my father and his crowd. And when my time came to kill or be killed, I didn't want to be around.

A few days later two policemen came to the house to talk to my father about credit cards stolen from a house in our neighborhood.

"Why do you keep doing this to us, coming here and accusing us?" I asked them, not concealing my surliness.

The older officer walked over. "Let me tell you something," he said softly. "We know your dad. You're not like him. You can be different if you wanna be."

"Yeah, maybe, but you don't live here."

"Ever thought about moving out?"

"Yeah, sure, where? But tell me something, how do you become a police officer?"

"Finish school."

"I don't like school."

"Then get your GED."

"What's that?"

"It's a diploma for people who don't like school."

A while later, the police officers left. I couldn't even tell Griff or Gina what I had asked the cop. They would have thought I was crazy—me, a cop? Impossible.

But no one knew how badly I wanted to get out of that house.

As much as I was trying to get away, Griff was moving closer to my father. He had bought into all my father's talk about becoming a real man by going to jail. Being a girl hadn't spared Gina, either. She was starting to hang out with a rough crowd.

My father must have sensed my growing coolness toward him—for he bought me a car. Lent it to me is more accurate, for a week later, he took it back.

Then a few weeks later he gave me another car, and I was as excited as when I got the first. And just as with the other car, my father took the second one back.

I was used to now-you-see-them-now-you-don't gifts. But my friends thought I was lying when I pulled up in my first new car and said it was mine—only to end up taking the bus to school a few days later. Then, to create total confusion, I came back with another car that soon disappeared the way the other had.

If I had told them about my father, they would have called me a bigger liar.

Out of the blue, my father started taking all of us on spur-of-the-moment trips to Hawaii. Usually we'd find out we were leaving about two hours before the late-night Pan American flight from San Francisco. He'd come into our rooms, rousing us, telling us to get dressed. "Let's go. We're going to Hawaii." Sometimes he was in such a hurry that Doris and Mandy didn't have time to change. They'd go to the airport in pajamas. My father would pay cash for all our tickets, get us buckled into our seats on the plane, and then go up to the cocktail lounge on the next level.

As soon as we got to Hawaii, he'd take us shopping for beach clothes. Everything was at break-neck speed, but I'd be lying to say it wasn't fun to go swimming on Waikiki Beach. My father would sit at a bar on the beach, keeping an eye on Griff and me, all the while making sure the baby sitter he'd hired was tending to Gina, Kelly, Doris, and Mandy.

My father believed in carrying a lot of cash. He usually kept it rolled up in a sock inside a shoulder bag.

One afternoon he took Griff and me sailing on an outrigger which the Hawaiian crewman told him never turned over. Ours did, and my father lost his bag. He offered the crewman fifty dollars to find the bag, but the man couldn't leave the boat.

When we got back to shore, my father told Griff and me to put on flippers and go back out.

At that moment, a man came wading out of the ocean, my father's bag over his shoulder. My father said it was his bag, took it back, looked inside, and saw the money was safe. He gave the man fifty dollars, went back to the beachfront bar, spread the sixty thousand dollars in wet hundred dollar bills across the wooden bar, and then sat back to sip Mai-Tais while letting the soaked bills dry.

There must have been half a dozen of those trips by the time I turned seventeen. Seven people flying at a moment's notice to Hawaii. Then new clothes for everyone. And three rooms at a top hotel. Food, drinks, tips—they all added up. But my father always had more than enough to pay in cash.

I couldn't believe he could earn as much money as he spent. Later, I learned I was right. When my mother died, each of the children inherited a one-hundred thousand dollar trust fund. "For our future," she had written in her will. With his friends in the county courthouse and the district attorneys, my father managed to come up with the right paper-work and judge's stamp, and to get power of attorney over our trusts. Whenever he needed money, he would type in the amount, stamp the document with the judge's signature, and then go down to the bank and withdraw forty thousand dollars at a time.

To make sure there wouldn't be any questions, he had gone down to the bank weeks before to charm the young and not-so-young tellers, now happy to give him "his money." In two years, he went through six hundred thousand dollars.

When I learned that neither my siblings nor I had any trust fund left, I thought, well, it's just another scam my father ran on six strangers: his children.

I had to move out. I knew I could never free myself from my father as long as I was living in his house. I would have to give up and start a new life away from him. But where? And when?

The next afternoon he was drinking when the police came to the front door. He walked out on the porch to talk with them.

A few minutes later, he came back in to say the bank had taken the house and we had twenty-four hours to move out. He got drunk and went to bed—while Griff and I went to rent a truck to load our furniture.

I knew I didn't want to be a part of another move. It would be the same thing all over again, only worse, the way a boat in a whirlpool is circling around and around, as though it's going somewhere but is only heading down to its own ruin.

Before my father woke, I left to San Francisco to enlist in the army. For once, I did as he had done: forging his signature to say, at seventeen, that I had his permission.

The enlistment sergeant promised that I would be trained at Fort Ord and be able to come home and see my family on weekends. He was either lying or had a weird sense of humor, for that night I was on a plane to Fort Polk, Louisiana for infantry training.

When he learned I had enlisted in the military, my father exploded. He telephoned me at camp, yelling that I was the lowest kind of person in the world: disloyal. I had betrayed him, he said, shouting obscenities and hanging up.

Training went well for a few months. Tricks I had learned in Marin paid off in the barracks. I started lending money at high interest, getting off-limits liquor and even finding ways to get women to drive out to the base, telling the MP at the gate they were my cousins. They were really coming to screw the recruits … for a price. Wheeling and dealing came easier now. The only thing I felt bad about was leaving Griff. I knew my father would take my leaving out on him, and I knew that Griff didn't know how to fight back against our father—or didn't want to. I had abandoned him.

After four months of training I was ordered to the captain's office. Keeping me standing at attention, the company commander informed me he had been contacted by Bank of America and told that I owed sixty thousand dollars on my credit cards. The captain warned me that I could face a court martial for purposefully accruing unpaid debts on my credit cards.

I swore I didn't know what he was talking about. The captain called the bank and put me on the phone with a banker who began reading off a list of charges, including three trips to Hawaii in the previous two months.

"I haven't been out of Louisiana since I got here four months ago," I said. "The army doesn't let soldiers leave training to go on vacation."

"You're Rudy J. Woolf, aren't you?" he snapped.

It took a lot of explaining on my part before the banker finally accepted my story that my father had taken out two credit cards in my name and was getting cash advances just below the maximum daily limit. My father hadn't stopped at cash either; he was using his connections to make purchases way over the credit limit.

When the banker finally hung up, the captain said he wanted to speak with my father. "He's jeopardizing your military career."

I didn't want to be charged with contempt by laughing in his face so I merely nodded. "Yes, sir. Maybe you had better explain that to him."

The captain reached my father at home. He hardly had time to explain why he was calling when my father started shouting, "Fuck you! Fuck you and the Army!"

My father's voice was so loud that the captain had to hold the phone away from his ear. We both stood listening as my father let out an unbroken stream of obscenities. Finally, the ranting stopped and he hung up.

"That's your father?" the captain asked, looking astonished.

"Yes, sir."

"With exactly the same name as yours?"

"Yes, sir."

A week later I was flying back to California. In my pocket was an Honorable Discharge Under Hardship Conditions in my pocket. The Army didn't want anyone in its ranks who had a father like mine, especially a criminal with the same name.

My father was gone when I got home. I was glad. I didn't want to fight with him. Gina had moved out since my departure and was now living with her boyfriend. I visited with Griff and my other sisters and waited for my father's return. I heard him yelling before I saw him run naked past the window. It was my father all right, chasing a half-dressed woman down the street. As he started up a neighbor's lawn, he wavered, grabbed for the porch, and then passed out on the grass.

I went outside and started to carry him home when a cop car pulled up. They got him dressed in the clothes he had left in his car and then took him to jail.

What a homecoming, I thought.

I took my father's car and drove down to San Rafael and pulled up at the locked gate of the cemetery where my mother was buried. I scaled the wall and went to find her grave.

When I found her, I sat down on the ground, trying to tell her how much I missed her. After a while, I felt better and went back to the car. For a few minutes I sat in the front seat, trying to figure out what to do. I turned on the radio and ran the dial over the different stations until hearing a tune I remembered from when I was a kid: "When You Wish Upon A Star."

Leaning out the window, I gazed up at the sky. It was overcast, and I couldn't find any stars. All the while I was listening to the song on the radio: "When you wish upon a star, makes no difference who you are …"

No star to wish on, I kept thinking. When the song ended, I left the cemetery.

Before returning the car, I stopped to call a friend who lived in Novato. Mark was the first openly gay man I had ever known. It wasn't something he had told me, but I could tell, for he never showed any interested in girls. But I didn't care. He had never tried to make a move on me, and I trusted him.

When I told Mark I had to find a place to stay right away, he said to come over that night and stay as long as I wanted.

Mark earned a living as a fence. People would bring him things; he'd pay them, and then he would sell them for more. While I was staying there, people were turning up at all hours of the night with cameras, radios, watches, and jewelry. Mark would quote a price and the thief would usually take it. Mark would stick whatever it was, microwave or electric typewriter, into his jammed closet, then go back to bed.

A week after I moved in, we drove over to San Francisco in his convertible. We started drinking and ended up in the Wax Museum. There we were, sloppy drunk, wandering past all these wax dummies of famous people. Walking ahead of me, Mark stopped in his tracks. "Look who's here," he said.

I glanced over. Frankenstein was standing in the corner. He looked pretty scary. Mark made sure the attendant wasn't in sight and then climbed over the stanchion and patted the monster on the chest. "I've had this thing for Frankenstein since I was a kid," he said. "Think he'd fit in the car?"

When I didn't answer, Mark climbed back over the stanchion. "Wait here. I'm going to tell the ticket guy that I left my wallet in the car. I'll be right back."

While I waited, a few people wandered by, probably thinking I was nuts, hanging out in front of the monster. Ten minutes later Mark came back. He looked round, then took out a rope and a hacksaw blade from under his windbreaker. "Tell me if anyone comes," he said. With that, he looped the rope around the head and started sawing off the head of Frankenstein. I don't know if it was the noise or if there was a hidden camera, but the lights came on. Mark yanked Frankenstein's head, and off it came off, bouncing to the floor. He grabbed the head and took off for the emergency exit, with me right behind him. As we hit the door, an alarm went off.

We sprinted up the alley with Frankenstein's head.

Leaping into the car, we sped off toward the Embarcadero. Mark wanted to throw the police off his track, so rather than take the Golden Gate Bridge back to

Novato, we took the long way around—over the Bay Bridge, then up the Nimitz Freeway, and across the Richmond—San Rafael. It was late, and there weren't many vehicles on the bridge. I kept glancing back over the long, flat span to see if there were any cops behind us.

Hearing me say it was clear, Mark floored the Blazer. We were racing over the bridge at more than 90 miles at hour, with the head of Frankenstein staring up from the back seat.

A blast of wind off the bay hit the side of the car and got under the convertible top. In an instant, it was torn away like cellophane paper—and we skidded to a stop beyond the bridge. We looked back. The top had blown over the side into Richardson Bay.

Turning, I saw massive walls in the distance and bright lights coming down on a large white sign: *San Quentin Prison.*

"Shit, Mark, let's get out of here, or we're gonna end up there."

A few months later Mark got busted for burglary. As it was his third felony conviction for theft, he was sent to San Quentin.

It took me a while longer.

-#-

4

Apparition in a 7-Eleven

It was difficult not to revert to the old ways of earning money. I wanted to find something that offered a decent wage. The trouble was I didn't have a high school diploma. What work I was offered paid little more than minimum wage. But I had to start somewhere.

I took a clerk position at 7-Eleven in Mill Valley. Standing at the counter, stuffing soft drinks and potato chips into a paper bag, I realized I was still a bag boy—but the old-fashioned kind. A few weeks later I started thinking about my misplaced dream of becoming a police officer. One afternoon I drove up to the San Rafael Police headquarters to see if I could start somewhere.

It felt strange walking into the police station. I knew most of the officers; more accurately, they knew my father, either from drinking with him in Marin County bars or handcuffing him when he'd gotten arrested for fighting or drunk driving.

Although the sergeant at the front desk seemed a little surprised to hear that one of the Woolfs wanted to become a policeman, he soon signed up me up as a cadet.

It was exciting work, helping the police photographer at crime scenes or referring people to the right place when they showed up with an emergency. The only drawback was the pay. It wasn't much more than 7—Eleven paid me. Even with the two salaries, I didn't have enough to get my own place.

Once Mark got arrested and lost his apartment, I needed to find another place to stay. I couldn't bring myself to ask my father to let me come back. And I was becoming claustrophobic inside the small room I had rented in San Francisco. My sister Gina came through. She told her boyfriend that I needed a place. They gave me a room in the back of their house, and I came and went as I wished. It was a new freedom, one I enjoyed—not waking to my father shaking me and ordering me down to the kitchen to scrub the floor, or waking to the sight of red lights flashing when the police would be called to our house for yet another family disturbance.

At first, it was quiet. Then things started to get loud and busy at night. All sorts of people were drifting by to stay for hours—bikers, mostly. Gina's boyfriend was older. I don't know if he introduced her to drugs, but she started using them. She seemed to have things under control at first. When I asked her why she was getting stoned so much, she told me it was just to relax. As for her getting drunk too, I couldn't talk. I was doing the same, more often than I liked. Booze seemed like a fast, cheap way of forgetting everything at once. And Gina had a lot to forget.

For instance, a few years after my mother's death, my father had bought Gina a horse. She kept it in the stable down the street, not far from the house we lived in then.

One day someone, we never learned who, shoved a broomstick up the horse's rectum and punctured its internal organs. Hemorrhaging, the horse broke out of the stable, lurching down the street toward our house. A groom called the house to tell Gina what had happened. She ran outside and saw her horse coming, blood dripping from its rear. She broke down, sobbing. My father heard all the commotion, looked outside, saw what was happening, and called the humane society. They told him they couldn't send someone right away. My father said he wasn't going to let the animal suffer, so he got his pistol and went outside. Gina was yelling and screaming, trying to calm the horse, now on its side in the street. Pulling Gina back, my father shot the horse in the head.

Minutes later, three squad cars pulled up, the cops getting out, threatening to arrest my father for killing the animal. The horse's body was blocking the street and the cops weren't able to drag it to the side. Finally, somebody called a tow company, which sent a flatbed truck. They hoisted the carcass on back and drove away, leaving Gina and a pool of blood in the middle of the street.

She never seemed the same after her horse died. It was like a light went off inside her, and she never wanted to turn it back on again or cared. Even though I was living in her house, I couldn't talk to her about her problems. I wasn't even able to understand my own.

One night, unable to sleep with the music blaring through the floor, I went down to 7-Eleven to hang out with the guy at the counter. I was in back getting ice cream out of the freezer when I looked over and saw a girl poking through the shelves next to me.

Slender with a pale complexion and blue eyes, she was wearing all black, including her hat which had a red floral design. I recognized her from high school.

"I know you, don't I?" I said.

"Oh, you're R.W.," she replied.

I smiled. She had called me by the nick-name I preferred, because it wasn't the nickname everybody called my father Rudy.

"I'm Amy," she said.

We kept talking all the way out into the parking lot. I felt good talking with Amy, and I didn't want her to leave. I wanted to invite her somewhere, but all I had in my pocket was five bucks. I took a chance and asked her to Denny's, where I had just enough money to buy her a cup of coffee and a piece of pie. I asked for a glass of water. The waitress must have felt sorry for me, for she gave me a coffee on the house.

We went back to my room and sat on the bed, talking and listening to Frank Sinatra records. I had never met anyone like Amy before. She listened to me when I talked, and made me feel as though I mattered. Being together that night wasn't about making love; it was about being together as long as we could be. I didn't want that night to end. I took her home early in the morning.

That same day, I telephoned and asked her to dinner. I got an advance on my paycheck and took her to Luca's in San Francisco. I wanted to go to a place where I would be greeted, and where Amy would see I wasn't just some dumb kid working at 7-Eleven. During dinner I couldn't help asking her if she had had a good time the night before.

She was so happy, she said, that after going home, she told her grandmother she had met the person she wanted to spend her life with.

Reaching over the red checkered tablecloth, I took her hand. "Amy, will you marry me?"

"Yes," she answered without a moment's hesitation.

Love at first sight sounds like a cliché. But every cliché contains a lost truth. Every part of my life changed once I met Amy. It was as though I had been walking backward. She turned me around so that I was facing my future—instead of staring at the past. Now, all around me, everything started blossoming. Well, almost everything.

I didn't dare tell my father about Amy. As for introducing them, I sensed it would be hopeless. Instinctively, I knew he would insult her and shower her with the foul language he used on every woman I had seen him with, even my mother. So I kept my secret about falling in love with Amy.

When I started to know Amy, I noticed something strange about both of us: We didn't talk about our families. I kept hoping that she would invite me back to meet her parents, and that I would find them happy together. By marrying Amy, I thought I could give up one bad family to inherit a good one.

I was wrong. Amy was as estranged from her mother as I was from my father. It wasn't fair, I thought, for two people from crazy families to fall in love.

Later, I realized that it was our vulnerability that formed the laws of attraction that drew us together. It never once occurred to me then that, at twenty, we were much too young to get married. We were desperate to flee our ruined families ... without realizing we were in greater danger of creating our own—just as sad, just as bad, just as mad.

As my family was ruled by violence and anger, Amy's was filled with guilt and hypocrisy. Unlike the patriarchy of my family, Amy lived in a matriarchy. Her father had initiated the divorce, leaving the mother to raise Amy and her siblings.

When I finally met Amy's mother, it was like hearing my father talking. All I had to do was change the sound of her voice, and it was the same angry talk. Amy's mother felt about men what my father did about women: good for one thing, sex.

Amy's mother had raised her to believe all men were out for one thing and one thing alone. If Amy was going to give it to them, then she better make sure it came at a price. Love never came into it. But Amy and I wanted more than anything what was missing from our two families: love. To have a chance, I knew we had to have our own home. She would have to leave her mother's house as I had left my father's.

Quitting 7-Eleven, I went to work as a sales representative at a toy company and then took a second job working nights as a tow truck driver. Realizing I still wasn't earning enough, I took on a third job as a security guard. Since the police cadet job didn't pay, I had to give it up. I regretted quitting, but knew I had to start earning enough money for a home and family of my own. Although I was starting to make sales and hold my own against the other reps at the toy company, I couldn't break into the big commissions. Something was missing from my technique. Time and time again, just when I was about to close a sale, it would slip away. It was as though by making my pitch, I had used up all my ability, and if the customer started showing some doubt about buying, I couldn't muster any more force to carry the sale off. I knew I could become a great salesman if I could only find out what was missing in my presentation. Everything was commission. No sales, no salary. With Amy depending on me, I had to master sales fast or get out of the business and find something steady.

One of the other reps told me about a super salesman in San Francisco who was going to give one of his motivation lectures. He said the guy was a legend, not just in the Bay Area but all over the country. With nothing to lose but the cost of the admission, I went to hear Norman Levine give a talk called "Believing Is Everything."

Mr. Levine was mesmerizing. He had an auditorium of top salespeople spellbound. I couldn't believe how well he spoke. It wasn't just his vocabulary, it was something else—eloquence mixed with self-confidence that wasn't at all conceited but totally self-assured. I had never heard anyone talk with such confidence. He seemed to understand everything there was to know about human behavior.

I had to discover the secret of his success so I could make it mine.

After he finished answering questions from the audience, I went out to the lobby to buy a tape of the lecture and then went home to absorb everything Mr. Levine had said.

A few days later, I decided to go see if he would talk to me. I knew it was naïve to think he would see me, and pushy, too, for believing I could talk myself into his office. I was afraid to telephone because I sensed he would hang up. I didn't dare write him—not with my sloppy penmanship and poor spelling. So I decided to go in person to his office on Montgomery Street in San Francisco. I guess I wasn't the first young salesperson to come in without an appointment to see Norman Levine. As soon as I asked to see him, his secretary was on her feet, saying he was in a meeting and showing me toward the door. But I kept insisting I had to see Mr. Levine.

He must have heard me saying I had to see him, for his door opened and he told his assistant it was all right. He would see me. His was the first posh office I'd ever been in. It wasn't just the expensive furniture or paintings that impressed me. It was the quality of everything I saw, from the crystal ashtray to the gold fountain pen. Here, I thought, is what success looks like. And to reinforce my impression, I noticed that one wall was covered with sales awards and photographs of Mr. Levine with celebrities.

Without even being asked, I started telling him about myself—probably too much and too personal, too—and about me dropping out of school and then getting into sales. I was scared to death to be telling him about my past, so I just kept telling him everything about myself, except not a word about my family. I even told him about starting to work in North Beach at thirteen, concealing that I had been my father's bag boy.

I went on to say that I thought I had a really good sense of character and was a pretty good salesman, but I lacked the polish the best sales representatives possessed. It was like they possessed magic words to whisper before making a sale, and I wanted to know what they were.

Mr. Levine finally motioned for me to stop. "I get the picture, young man. I can see you've got what it takes—but you're just starting off and, to be honest, you're a little rough around the edges. But believe me, you have the talent. I can see it. I meet hundreds of salesmen all the time, and I can always tell the ones who can become great and those who can't."

"What's the difference between them, Mr. Levine? What's the secret?"

He smiled. "It's no secret. Everybody knows it; they don't believe it."

"Believe what?"

"In yourself."

Maybe I looked as though I were waiting for more, for he held up his hand. "I know, it sounds too easy. But if you don't have it, you won't be able to sell fire to a freezing man, but if you have it, you can sell whatever you want." He glanced at his watch and got up. "I have a luncheon date, but believe me. Believe in yourself. You'll see it'll make every bit of difference to you and the world."

I left while he was talking with his secretary. I wanted to ask how I went about believing in myself, but I knew I couldn't ask for more of his time. I would have to find out on my own.

The next couple weeks I tried to show clients that I believed in myself. But my sales didn't change. I made a few, as I always did, but I wasn't making the big sales. They were still eluding me. Mr. Levine's advice was like a box filled with treasure that I couldn't open. So I put it aside and went about finding work that didn't depend on me believing in myself. I had nine different jobs in six months, trying to find the one that would give me the salary and benefits I needed to have in order to be a good husband.

As the day of my wedding approached, though, I knew I couldn't keep hiding Amy from my family. I had to tell them. They were part of me as I was part of them.

I was amazed at the response I received. Gina was too stoned to care; Griff was in and out of juvenile hall and trying to score his own drugs; Kelly was growing into a private secretary for my father, walking around, saying, "Yes, Daddy. Yes, Daddy"; and Doris and Mandy were too young to experience the numbness and pain the older children had inherited. As for my father, he couldn't believe I was getting married for a "piece of ass." He didn't understand or care that I had fallen in love with Amy.

Soon, though, I had enough money for Amy and me to get a small apartment in San Rafael. It wasn't much but it was ours. We bought an old Toyota with a passenger window that would never close and a heater that didn't work. But we'd throw a blanket over our laps and drive to the ocean at Stinson Beach to watch the sun come up.

I was happier than I had ever been, and I think Amy was too. We had escaped our families. We were free now. But there was much I didn't know about living together. I had to change my lifestyle, like when I wanted to go out and drink with my buddies and I knew Amy didn't drink and didn't like going out. I began to discover that we didn't have a lot in common, but I figured with time we'd sand down our differences and become alike.

Then the wedding day. From Amy's side of the family, only her mother came. From my side, my father, my siblings, and my aunt attended.

Amy and I were both nervous. We wanted everything to go right, even if we didn't know how to do it. We just wanted to make it a day we never forgot.

My father also wanted to make sure I would never forget my wedding. It wouldn't have been enough just to get drunk and come on to one of the guests. No, he had to go much deeper to find something to contribute to that event. His gaze settled on the one person present who was the figurehead for Amy's world as he was for mine. In spite of all her professed disgust for men, Amy's mother was unable to resist the charms of my father.

They went off together and soon, hard as it was for me to believe, were screwing in some motel room.

I never would have known about it—if my father hadn't bragged about it to me.

He waited months for the right moment—when we were in the midst of an argument about me spending my free time with Amy.

"She's just a whore like her mother."

"Shut up!," I yelled. "You don't know what you're talking about."

"Don't I? I balled her mother at the wedding, Rudy Boy."

As horrible as it sounded, I sensed it was true. Who else but my father would violate every rule of civility and protocol to get what he wanted—especially if it gave him a secret that he could use against me at a later date? He loved accumulating secrets that would turn poisonous with time. Then he would reveal them to me.

I tried to keep away from him, from Gina, from Griff, from everyone who reminded me of the past. I wanted to concentrate on the future with Amy.

Sensing we knew little about the responsibilities of having a family, we decided to wait before having children. Needless to say, Amy got pregnant within two months of the marriage. Things are serious now, I realized. I'm going to be a father.

Amy did a better job of being a wife than I did as a husband. I couldn't stop worrying about money, or the lack of it. I'd get short of cash and start to work one of my deals—boosting auto parts or scalping sporting event tickets. I told her the extra money came from sales commissions at work. And Amy believed me. It hurt, because I lied so easily. I was good at lying. It just came naturally, learning to cover up for myself, for my family, for my friends. But now I was lying to my wife—and I felt bad, but I wasn't strong enough to tell her the truth about where I had been and what I had done. I kept telling myself things were going get better; then there wouldn't be any need for lies. Money took the place of communication with Amy. I could stay out late, then come home with cash I could put in front of her, saying, "Here, this is for you and the baby."

Yet, when our daughter Gail was born in San Rafael and I went to see Amy in her hospital room, I got scared, seeing her holding this tiny little face looking at me. I drove over to San Francisco, had dinner and a few drinks, all the while leaving Amy alone in the hospital. Maybe that's when Amy started erecting a wall between us. I had enough walls inside me not to notice another one going up, even if it was between me and the person I loved most in the world.

The cost of a family was growing faster than my ability to earn a living. My sales were fluctuating—one good week, one bad—and driving the tow truck meant hours with low pay. I needed to find a job with good pay, and more important, with decent medical insurance for Amy and Gail.

More money was needed, and I didn't know where to get it legally.

Then the rest of the ceiling came down on me.

My father had filed tax returns listing Amy and me as his dependents. If that wasn't lie enough, he wrote that we had had a baby that died at birth, and that he had paid all the medical and funeral expenses.

Amy couldn't believe what he had done and she wanted me to confront him. I knew it wouldn't do any good.

Credit card statements in my name started arriving at our apartment. All were signed Rudy J. Woolf, with his signature above my address. My father had reverted to what he had done after his father's death and after I had joined the army: forging documents in the name of Rudy J. Woolf—me, not him.

Amy wanted me to prosecute my father. But I couldn't.

We went bankrupt. Amy lost all respect for me. She couldn't believe that I wouldn't stand up for myself, let alone her and Gail. But my father was still the strongest force in my life—stronger than anyone, Amy or Gail, most of all me. Amy said she was going to file for divorce and wanted me to move out.

I moved back in with my aunt and continued with my different jobs, giving all I could to Amy and the baby. But every time I went to see her, she made me feel as though I was a stranger. I had to win back her respect, and what I had never had—my own. Every time, it seemed that she was beginning to trust me, though, I would let her down.

My aunt was having a family gathering and insisted I bring Amy. I didn't want to, but I thought maybe, just maybe, everything would go right.

The party was a disaster, not because of my father for once—but because of me. Amy wore the heart-shaped diamond I had given her. When Gina saw it dangling from a silver chain on Amy's neck, she told her to take it off. "That's my necklace," she exclaimed. It was true. I didn't know it but when I stole the necklace from Griff, he had already swiped it from Gina. I was so stupid, I thought the diamond had come from one of Griff's burglaries; instead, it was my sister's; and now my wife was humiliated that I had given her stolen property, stolen from my own family. I only wanted to give Amy something nice, something I couldn't afford, so I stole it. I was still using the old ways to work things out. And the old ways were rapidly destroying what was left of Amy's love for me.

My life resembled a scramble of pieces from different jigsaw puzzles. Nothing matched anything else. To get close again with Amy, I knew I'd have to throw everything out and start from scratch. I decided to follow through on becoming a cop. A few days later, I went to the San Rafael Police Department and said I wanted to apply to be a police officer. I should have expected the reaction. The lieutenant on duty took me aside to say I could never be an officer in their department. He told me everyone on the force knew my father, one way or another. I could never be trusted, he said. If there was a problem involving my father, no one would know which side I would stand on.

"You gotta cut your ties," he said, "but you can't do it here."

I couldn't believe what he was telling me. I'd been so careful never to be arrested. And now I was locked out of becoming a cop. The lieutenant must have seen that I was taking it hard, for he told me that he heard Richmond was hiring officers.

Richmond was a tough industrial town on the other side of San Francisco Bay. I didn't want to be a cop there. I wanted to be a cop in the area where I grew up. But I knew nothing I could say would make a difference.

Rudy J. Woolf had sealed shut one more door for me.

I drove to Richmond.

I guess I was lucky to have found a sympathetic cop. He probably saved me a lot of time filling out forms and waiting for an interview. After I stopped at the main desk and asked about a job application, the gray-haired sergeant looked around and leaned over the counter. "You didn't hear this from me, kid, but you're not the right color."

"Huh?" I said.

Seeing I didn't understand, he pointed at my black shirt. "Gotta be like that, or yellow or brown. We got a quota now. Come back in six months and maybe there'll be an opening for you."

All my hopes for being a police officer seemed to vanish in that lobby.

As I came up the grade from the Richmond—San Rafael Bridge, I noticed the blaze of lights beside the bay. A long wedge of grim buildings appeared in the distance: San Quentin Prison.

"What the hell?" I thought, maybe they're hiring guards.

Pulling off the highway, I went down the road until I saw a gate with a uniformed guard watching me. I parked and walked over to him. "Are they hiring here?" I asked.

He looked me up and down. "As a guard or an inmate?" he said, without smiling.

"I mean it. Can I fill out an application?"

He studied me a few seconds. Then his stance softened. "You don't look like you're tough enough to make it in here. But the personnel office is open in the morning if you wanna come back."

I thanked him and returned to the car, pausing to glance over at the prison. In the darkness, the buildings seemed to dominate the landscape like an enormous castle. On the drive back to Marin, I kept wondering if there was much difference between being a police officer and a prison guard.

The following morning I drove over to the prison and asked for an application. I filled it out on the spot and left to wait word if I would be hired.

Ten days later, Amy telephoned my sales office to say I had received a letter from San Quentin. I had used her address on the application. I didn't want the hiring committee to know I was having marital difficulties. The letter gave me a date and time for my first interview. I was excited about being hired. Amy definitely wasn't. She was unable to understand how badly I wanted a job with security for her and Gail.

When I drove over to get the letter, Amy showed me the divorce papers she hadn't mailed yet. For weeks she had been holding on, waiting to see if I would change. All the papers needed was her signature and she would be divorced from me. Even though she had talked about divorcing me, I didn't think she would go through with it. I was scared and must have showed it.

She invited me to stay for dinner. We didn't argue that night. Instead, we played with Gail, and I think we were just happy to be a family again—no matter for how brief a time. Maybe Amy saw something different in me that night. I don't know what it was. Maybe she sensed I was trying to pull my life together because she asked me to move back with her and Gail.

That night we burned the divorce papers in the sink. Three weeks later I went for my interview at San Quentin.

-#-

5

Going Inside

When I arrived at the administration building at San Quentin, I found more than a hundred other men and women also applying to be prison guards. After completing a lengthy application, we had to take an SAT. I was worried about passing. I had never been strong in math, and at that time my spelling and grammar were shaky.

After lunch break, we were broken into groups and told to wait for our background interview. I later learned someone had already done a background check with the San Rafael Police Department. The officer who contacted them said he was calling from San Quentin and checking on Rudy Woolf. Whoever took the call asked, "What's he in for?"

It took a few minutes to clear up the confusion by checking my date of birth. There was a lot of joking when the police in San Rafael found out that it wasn't my father arriving there to serve a sentence but his son trying to get a job as a guard.

There wasn't any joking, though, when I went into the interview room and found three guard officers and two administrators waiting. Maybe they were tired from asking the same questions all day, but I didn't see one smile or hear one remark to make me feel at ease. It was all very serious. I felt as though I was on trial to prove myself. They asked me all sorts of questions about my background—but the only one that mattered was, "Have you ever been arrested?"

I answered honestly, "No."

Later, I thought about it. What if they had asked, "Have you ever committed a crime?" I still would have answered no, telling myself it wasn't a lie. I had never committed a crime in the eyes of the law because I had never been tried for any of the things I had done against the law.

When I got home that night, Amy said I had gotten an urgent message from my father. Gina had been kidnapped. I called my father. He said to come right over. A ransom note had arrived and he had called his buddies at the police department. By the time I got to his house, three FBI agents from the San Francisco branch had already set up listening devices on the phone.

We waited several hours. Finally, I had to get back to Amy and couldn't wait any longer for the call from the kidnappers. It came an hour after I left. My father telephoned later, laughing. He said some guy had called to say he was holding Gina hostage, and he wanted ten thousand dollars in ones and fives or he was gonna kill Gina.

"Kill her," my father said, and then hung up on the caller.

"Are you crazy?" I shouted. "They'll kill Gina."

"Bullshit! He's one of Gina's biker friends trying to hustle me for money. No real kidnapper is gonna ask for ten grand in ones and fives. He's a fuckin' punk."

He was right. The next day Gina was "released" without a cent of ransom being paid. The FBI didn't appreciate her little stunt and was going to arrest her for arranging her own abduction.

My father used his connections to get Gina out of the country, to Venezuela, where she could stay with his friends until things had calmed down.

As for Griff, he was fast rivaling my father for the highest number of arrests. Busted for dealing drugs, he had moved deeper into the state judicial system—going from juvenile hall in Marin County to the California Youth Authority at Preston, one arrest away from adult prison.

I couldn't save my siblings. I could only try to save myself.

Six weeks later, I was called back to San Quentin for a second interview.

Amy had been hoping I hadn't made it past the first interview, but when she realized they might be interested in hiring me as a guard, she got worried. She said that I was going to change if I went to work in a prison. She begged me not to go, even going so far as to tell me I should be a bag boy in North Beach again. But I wasn't turning back. Besides, I needed medical insurance. Amy was losing a lot of weight and she needed medical tests to find out what was wrong.

I returned to San Quentin.

Out of more than one hundred applicants, only sixty-seven were called back. Somehow I had passed the written test and the background evaluation. "Now for the next hurdle," I thought. I underwent a physical examination. Then I was told to go for my psychological interview. Again, the ranks had thinned. Only thirty-seven people were lined up when I came down the hall. One by one, they were called into the office, and one by one they left, without a word.

Finally, late in the afternoon, my turn came.

The interview room was sparse, with only a chair in the center of the room, and, at the far end, a long table behind which six men and a woman sat in correctional officers' uniforms. Just like at the first interview, there wasn't a friendly face in the room. The woman motioned for me to sit down.

I was sweating, but I didn't want to reach up and wipe my face and let them know how nervous I was. I just sat motionless, waiting.

Finally, one of the older officers cleaned his throat and leaned forward. "Mr. Woolf, how do you feel about incarcerated people?"

"Well, I guess they're here because they broke the law and present a risk to society."

My answer must have broken the ice, for they started asking me all sorts of general questions, ranging from my philosophy of life to what sports I had played in high school. Then whap, just as I was getting relaxed, they started hitting me with hard questions: How did I feel about firearms? Did I believe in the death penalty? Did I think even the worst person was capable of changing?

I answered the best I could. Yes, I believed in firearms; yes, I was in favor of capital punishment; but I also believed even the worst person could change.

After about an hour, they told me that I had completed the second portion of the oral interview, and I was to go down the hall for a follow up on my background.

There were two lieutenants waiting. They only had one question: How did I feel about my father?

I didn't think about the answer. I just said what came into my mind. "What do you mean, how do I feel about my father? He's my father. I love him."

"Of course," said one of the correctional officers. "We mean how do you feel about him as a person?"

I could see where they were going and decided to save them time. "Look, I know he's been in trouble with the law. But that's his life, not mine."

"So, you don't feel there's any danger of your being put into conflict with him if you were a law enforcement officer?"

"I came here because I wanted to be a prison guard. My father stopped having control over me a long time ago. I'm my own man."

"You're absolutely certain that if it came down to a question of loyalty between your father and loyalty to your fellow officers...."

"No question," I interrupted. "I'd stick with my fellow officers."

"How can you be sure?"

"I grew up in Marin County. I know this is a maximum security prison. I saw the gun towers coming in. I know that everyone's life around here, the guards' that is, depends on loyalty."

They didn't ask anymore questions. Then one of them told me to go over to the Administration Building. When I walked inside, I saw that the group of candidates had been whittled down to twenty-seven.

I waited as four or five men were called in for the next part of the interview process.

Finally, the door opened and someone called "Rudy J. Woolf."

Another group of officers was waiting. They didn't waste time on formalities or asking easy questions about what I thought about life. One started by asking, "What would you do if you saw an inmate stealing a knife in the kitchen?"

"I'd take the knife and isolate the inmate," I replied.

"And if he wouldn't give up the knife?"

"I'd call for help." I studied the faces. No one looked surprised or disappointed by my answer.

"Okay, Rudy," said the woman, "A guy's climbing up the wall. What are you going to do?"

I was momentarily startled to be called by my first name, but then tried to focus on the question. I could feel everyone staring at me, waiting for my answer. "Well, I'm not sure what the procedures are, but common sense would dictate that I should fire a warning shot."

"Why are you going to shoot a warning shot?" snapped an older officer with a tobacco-stained moustache.

"Ah, because you never wanna shoot at a person unless you're ready to shoot to kill."

"Wait a minute," he said, pointing his index finger at me. "You're giving me this bullshit stuff, and all the time the guy's scaling the wall."

I felt myself get hot. I didn't like his tone and that wagging finger. But I remembered what my father had always said: Keep people off balance by keeping them upset.

It wouldn't happen to me, not now, not here. "Well, I would stand there and monitor him. I mean, maybe he's gonna fall."

"Rudy, the guy's almost to the top of the wall, only a few feet more to go. What are you going to do?"

I sensed the woman officer trying to help me. But I didn't want the older officer to think he had intimidated me. I looked him in the eyes as though he had asked the question. "The guy's not going over the wall."

"What are you gonna do to stop him?" someone else asked.

"If the guy gets within two feet of the top of the wall, he's dead. I'm gonna shoot him right off the wall, and I'm not going to wound him. I'm going to shoot to kill. He's had every opportunity to stop. He's had people yelling at him to stop. I've given him warnings and let him know I'm armed and ready to take action. So he didn't listen. And I had to shoot him." I paused, looking down at the floor.

All the examiners leaned forward, staring down as though the make-believe inmate they had been using to test me was now lying dead on the floor.

Within five minutes I was dismissed and told to report the following morning at eight o'clock. When the woman officer escorted me back to the entrance, I couldn't help asking her if it looked like I was going get hired.

"Ask me no questions, I'll tell you no lies," she said with a straight face, and then grinned. "Be here at eight, though, or we'll lock the gates."

I was in the parking lot at 6 a.m.

Only nineteen of us were left to file into the administration building. The associate warden arrived to congratulate us for passing the exams and background checks. He said we would have the honor of being members of the first class of the California Correctional Officers Academy, which had just been opened at Folsom prison.

Other successful candidates would also be coming from Soledad, Pleasant Valley, and other correctional institutions throughout the state. Until we passed the Academy, we would be hired as temporary correctional officers and given a small salary for our living expenses at the Academy.

The associate warden swore us in as law enforcement officers and wished us luck at Folsom. Over half of the applicants were expected to flunk out, he added.

I wasn't worried. I had made it through the background test and the psychological evaluation. If I hadn't been eliminated because of my father's police record and my responses to the pass-or-fail questions, a three-week mini boot camp wouldn't stop me.

After being issued sweat suits and underwear to wear at the Academy, I was told to buy two uniforms with my own money. I would have to borrow it. I didn't want the people at San Quentin to know how broke I was.

As soon as I told Amy the good news, she started telling me I was going to change—for the worse. She was sure I would be hardened by the training at the Academy, and hardened even more at San Quentin. I promised that I wasn't going to let being a guard get to me. She didn't believe me, saying I couldn't work around murderers, thieves, and rapists without having some of their evil come off on me.

"Don't worry," I told her. I had made it through being a bag boy in North Beach at thirteen and never was destroyed by all the things my father had done. It didn't matter what I said to Amy. She was already dead certain that I was going to come back from Folsom a different man.

I laughed, telling her I hadn't even started yet.

If Amy's response to my job was fear, my father's was ridicule. When he realized I was serious about going to the Correctional Officers Academy then starting at San Quentin, he started laughing. "You're going to get eaten alive by those motherfuckers."

I ignored him.

As the time drew closer to leave for Folsom, my father must have realized I was serious, because he quit calling to put me down. Instead, he telephoned to tell me about friends he had behind the walls and things he wanted me to do for them. I couldn't believe it. I hadn't even started and I was already experiencing that tug of loyalty that the correctional officer had questioned me about.

"I won't do it," I told him when he said he wanted to get a letter inside to an old buddy at Folsom.

"Fuck you," he yelled, slamming down the phone so hard it hurt my ear.

Great encouragement for the future, I thought. My wife believes I'm going to become a monster and my father tells me to get fucked.

The next morning I packed my suitcase and said goodbye to Amy and Gail.

Folsom prison was picked as the site of the Correctional Officers Academy because of its proximity to Sacramento. Officials of the California Department of Corrections could drive over and see how the uneducated guards of the past were making way for the trained correctional officers of the future. Folsom was also selected because it was one of the state's oldest prisons. Four different facilities were located there, each with its own level of security within the main prison. Students at the Academy could experience the full range of penitentiary life. The professional improvements sounded good. I believed it. In fact, if anyone had asked me to come up with three words to describe a prison guard, I would have answered, "stupid," "dumb," "brutal." Not one would apply to me. I was going to be part of a new model of law enforcement. I was going to treat the men of San Quentin not as prisoners but as inmates—human beings who had made a mistake in society and were being rehabilitated behind bars.

The only trouble was that San Quentin was a Level IV prison. There was no higher level of security. Pelican Bay hadn't been constructed yet. San Quentin was where the worst of the worst were sent. An inmate just didn't arrive there from court after being sentenced for the first time. He had to earn his way to the cream-colored collection of fortless-like buildings at the north end of San Francisco Bay.

Correctional officers, though, were treated differently. They didn't have to serve first in a minimum prison, learning the ways in a world of little risk, before moving up to a medium prison, and then on to a maximum unit, and finally into a max A—with its prison within the prison, Adjustment Center, lock-down Maintenance Housing and Security Housing blocks, and Death Row—the end of the road at the end of the road. Before the Academy began, a new guard could go straight from being hired to turning up in uniform to begin walking the cell blocks—hoping that a kindly guard would take the time to point out who was to be watched and what to look for in the yard just before a riot.

I was luckier than the guards who had started their careers before I did. I was going to have three weeks of instruction before returning to patrol the sunless corridors of a compressed hell.

Arriving in the town of Folsom, we found ourselves assigned three to a room at the Folsom Inn. The Academy started the next morning, and for the next three weeks we attended classes during the day and then went bar-hopping at night. Every evening when we finished at the Academy, the party would start again. In fact, it was like one three-week party.

Some nights I would have to pull a pillow over my head to drown out the moans of my roommate screwing a woman he had picked up at a bar, or else I'd find myself taking a cold shower at dawn to clear my head from partying all night myself.

But at the Academy itself everyone got serious. We had classes that covered every aspect of being a correctional officer—from learning the California Penal code to self-defense. Officials at the Department of Corrections had two problems: one, image, the other, attrition. By creating the Academy, they thought it could solve both problems at once by transforming the perception of dumb goons with Rudy-clubs into intelligent young men and women given professional training to help them handle things. As for the increasing number of guards quitting over low pay and poor benefits, the Department of Corrections was raising salaries and offering better health and retirement packages that would make being a correctional officer comparable with employment at other law enforcement agencies.

But first we had to graduate from the Academy. Guards with years of experience and civil servants with graduate degrees taught us everything they knew about prisons and prisoners or, as we were to refer to them, institutions and inmates. We learned how to search a cell and how to read the different kinds of gang tattoos. A lot of time was spent familiarizing ourselves with weapons used by correctional officers. We fired the Mini-14 used on the gun towers and gun rails; we got to know the shotgun and the .38 revolver.

Every morning there would be a hole to close in the formation. Someone had quit or been dropped. A couple of students were even caught with drugs and were immediately dismissed from the Academy.

I didn't have any problem with physical training or taking orders. The Correctional Officers Academy reminded me of an easy-going Army boot camp.

I simply hadn't realized how extensive was the knowledge required to be a correctional officer. Under supervision, I visited Folsom cells and learned how to look for drugs, signs of drug use, and drug paraphernalia. I was shown how to protect a crime scene. I learned about the numerous gangs inside the California prisons, and the codes and slang used by each. I learned all the rules of staff-inmate relations. Much time was spent teaching the candidates about the different levels of security: from Level I, where inmates were able to live in dormitories and work unguarded, up through Level II and Level III, to the highest level, IV. Yet IV contained its own hierarchy of security.

We memorized not only the written rules but the unwritten ones, like when a sergeant told us never to put our hands on an inmate in front of people not in our unit.

"What if he spits on us?" asked my roommate.

"Just smile and say, 'We'll take care of this later.'"

The same day one of the female students accidentally fired an M-14 over an instructor's head at the rifle range. She was packed and gone by the time we got back to town.

Every night I called Amy, checking in to see how she and Gail were doing. I could tell she had been hoping I would flunk out or quit, but when she heard I was going to graduate and start working at San Quentin, all her worrying magnified.

She told me about meeting a nurse who worked at Marin General Hospital. The woman was always talking about guards being brought over after being injured by inmates.

"Amy, don't listen to her. Anyone can get hurt on the job."

"But look where you're gonna be working. I remember news on TV about guards being killed at San Quentin."

What could I say? It was true. During one of our classes, an instructor told us how George Jackson and other inmates had taken over the San Quentin Adjustment Center and killed three guards using fingernail clippers to tear out their jugular veins.

Everybody in class got real quiet. I told myself, I'm not going to get hurt at San Quentin. I'm not going to end up a statistic. Maybe it was so silent because everybody else was telling himself the same thing. As graduation day approached, I almost dreaded finishing the academy and going back home. I'm not sure what concerned me more: trying to deal with Amy's fears of my working at San Quentin, or my own. I couldn't even put the fear into words. Maybe it was coming into contact with thousands of men as ruthless as my father; or, maybe I was afraid that by stepping behind the walls as a correctional officer, I was sentencing myself to prison, too.

-#-

6

Beginning with Q

The first morning I was to start at San Quentin, Amy got up with me at 4 a.m. so we could talk, yet she fell silent watching me dress in my Department of Corrections uniform. I tried to explain that I now had a job that was going to supply with me with a good salary, and that I would be receiving full medical and dental coverage. All the previous jobs I had were either part-time, under-paid, or commission-based. Now we were totally protected. The insurance was our safety net. Amy constantly needed tests and medicine; Gail wasn't as strong as she should have been. She had all the illnesses that children get growing up—but she kept having relapses. I didn't know about the effects of stress in children, but Gail had been present when Amy and I would fight. Sometimes I would come home drunk and rather than play with her, I would go to sleep and then be gone again in the morning when she woke.

Amy wasn't only worried about my working at a prison; she was afraid that I was going to get trapped in being a correctional officer. I promised her that I was only going to be there for the minimal time before transferring laterally into a police department or probation officer's position—two years at most. No way was I going to stay behind the walls of San Quentin longer than I needed.

Then I left to begin my first shift. If I had known then what I was going to experience as a prison guard, I would have gone back to 7-Eleven, anything rather than sentence myself to more than years on the tiers.

No arrival ceremony awaited me. No veteran officer took me aside to tell me the way through the maze I stood before. I was merely told where to relieve the officer on duty, and then I started through the first of five steel doors leading inside the prison. As each one locked behind me and I waited for another to click open, I found myself standing in a kind of nowhere—suspended between the world outside and the world inside.

Finally, the last door, really more a vault, opened, and I was truly deeper into the core of the prison, for even though I could see the sky above me, it was pushed away by the walls towering over me. Everything was still, hushed, as though holding its breath—while I could feel my heart beating and hear my footsteps on the gravel path leading past a cell block. I've been through worse than this, I told myself, walking between rows of flowers that seemed out of place in the midst of a maximum security prison. I paused to glance up at the gun tower and the officer clutching a rifle, staring at me. I reached the corner and turned—then froze, ready to run.

Before me, in a shifting sea of light and dark blue, were hundreds and hundreds of men milling around in a large yard dominated by high walls from which more armed guards peered down. I glanced at a yellow line of paint running from where I stood, down the wall and back along the far side, and around the other side again: the dead line no inmate could cross without the risk of being shot. Stenciled in black on the wall: NO WARNING SHOT

More than anything I wanted to turn and hurry back through all the doors of the prison and go home, to tell Amy she was right. Being a correctional officer wasn't for me.

"Jesus Christ," I thought, "how the hell did I ever get here?"

By most accounts, I should have already been inside that swarm of blue-clad bodies in front of me. I knew there were men inside the walls who had done far less to end up here than I had. If there had been justice for all in the world, I would have been wearing prison garb at that moment. Standing there, I could feel the inmates glancing over—staring at me as though seeing, even smelling, my fear. They could probably tell from my pressed uniform and shiny badge that I was new. Some might even have guessed I was starting my first day. But if they didn't know, I sure wasn't going to tell them. It wasn't just my clothing that told the inmates I hadn't been inside the walls before. Nervousness must have been oozing out of me.

I started forward, heading toward the guard in a beige shirt and green trousers. He was walking toward me inside two more yellow lines that cut across the middle of the yard.

He, too, looked out of place—as though he didn't belong and now could leave. I glanced down at the whistle pinned to my shirt. The only thing I had to call for help. Could I get to it in time if I were attacked? Then I glanced up at the gunman on the tier. As though he knew I would be looking up and thinking I would be protected by his presence, he turned and walked away down the railing.

I moved into the milling crowd, not avoiding the hard stares, yet not staring back either. I just kept walking, sensing that if I fell, like a hunter in the midst of a herd of buffalo, I would be trampled to death.

No one blocked my path or said a word. No one moved either; they simply shifted to take me in—me, the new correctional officer, fresh out of the Academy. I paused to look back at where I had come from. The path seemed to vanish behind a wall of bodies.

"Hey, man, what you looking at?" someone said.

I shifted my gaze, taking in a massive black man whose mammoth arms were folded across his chest. "You think you're better than us?"

Several inmates glanced over, waiting for my reply.

"No, the only difference between you and me is that you got caught," I replied, starting away inside the fragile protection of the yellow lanes.

All during my first shift from seven in the morning to three in the afternoon, I kept being rotated to a different area of responsibility. After an interminable time, I got an hour break from patrolling the South Yard before being sent to the In-Service Training, where officers showed me the high-security Upper Yard and how to respond to the different cell blocks and, most of all, how to fulfill my primary job—keeping the inmates under control.

I learned how to escort an inmate along the wall so that the gunmen on the railing could protect me. Once, when I put my hand into my pocket, a sergeant struck me hard in the chest. "That's to remind you never to put your hand into your pocket. You're easier to attack when you only have one hand. And it also tells the inmates you're bored. These are predators, Woolf. They're always looking for prey. Don't give them any signs that leave you open."

"Is there a list of all the things not to do inside?" I asked.

"Hundreds of them, but they're not written down, except for the big ones, like sleeping in the towers, or bringing in contraband. You learn all the other rules on the job. Watch the inmates. They're the best teachers; of course, they're unforgiving, too. You only need to make a mistake once."

I could feel a chill mixing from the sweat soaking my T-shirt.

A few minutes later, I was shown through the furniture shop and the metal shop and the gym in the Lower Yard. The Lower Yard, where I had started, was for the general prison population. Even though San Quentin was a Level IV prison, it had two to three thousand inmates at other levels in the prison who were allowed to mingle together. They weren't considered a high risk either for the officers or the other inmates. Roughly half of San Quentin's seven thousand inmates Level IV, considered dangerous enough to be locked inside cells and only permitted out into the Upper Yard, which itself was divided into three areas to keep warring gangs separated when they were allowed outside. The Upper Yard sounded like no man's land and I wasn't ready yet to venture into it. I was happy the staff had decided to start me off in the Lower Yard.

Later in the afternoon, one of the officers took me up on the gun railing to look down at the mass of men milling in the yard. "What do you see down there?"

I wasn't sure what he meant, so I didn't answer.

"It's all about colors and color … if you get what I mean. See the red socks? That's the Crips. The blues, those are Bloods. Those whites over there are with Aryan Nation."

At the Academy, we had been lectured on gangs and had been shown training films on their organization. But here, looking down at the different clumps of blacks, of whites, of Hispanics, I felt like I was witnessing the survivors of some enormous shipwreck, huddled together for survival—and I was washed up with them.

"What do you see wrong about that mix over there?" the officer asked, pointing at two Hispanic inmates and two heavily tattooed inmates talking together.

"They look okay to me."

"Look closer. They're negotiating. That's a captain and a lieutenant from the Mexican gang and the heads of the biker gang maybe planning on killing a black, or a white, or another Mexican, and where the other gangs are going to fall in when they kill this guy. One gang doesn't wanna piss off the others, cause then they'll come back to kill a guy from the first gang, so they're working it out."

"Can't you break them up?"

"No, we can't prove anything right now. Have to wait till we toss their cells and find the weapon they're gonna use."

"Why not just keep the gangs isolated in different prisons?"

He laughed. "We don't have that many prisons. You got thousands of gang members spread through the state prison system, and a hell of a lot more outside."

Only a sociologist could have understood the complexity of the gang system within the walls. There were Native American gangs, white gangs, black gangs, Asian gangs, and Southwest Asian gangs. Usually, they stayed within their own subculture, but when racial fights broke out, colors merged together, fighting against all the other races. Keeping the truce among the gangs was essential for the security of all—guards and inmates. After a couple of hours, the inmates were escorted back to their cell blocks. Two other officers and I did body-searches of the inmates leaving the yard. It was one aspect of the job I felt uncomfortable about—frisking a man's body, especially in his crotch. But it came with the territory. I had to do it.

Everything was going fine until a wiry Hispanic inmate moved up in the line, with his pants tugged down around his ass, preventing me from checking his groin area for weapons.

I motioned for him to pull up his pants, but he wasn't going to be cooperative. I could see the inmates watching me, waiting to see what the new guard was going to do.

From the first day at the Academy, every officer had hammered home the same fundamental rule: Never ever let the inmates think you are not going "to hold your mud or hold your shit together."

"They'll always be testing you, especially at the start of your career," a sergeant told me. "And if they see you back down, you might as well quit on the spot. They'll look at you like their bitch, like some inmate who didn't put up a fight the first night in the block, even though he was gonna get his ass kicked. Now he's going get fucked in the ass by anybody who wants him … 'cause he didn't earn their respect and hold on to his own."

Again I motioned for the inmate to pull up his pants. "No, man, I want her to search me," he said, nodding toward the female officer patting down inmates in the next row.

"Hey, get up here," I ordered him. "I can go wash my hands with Dove soap so that my hands are nice and fresh and soft when I search you down. But right now get your pants up."

He didn't move. "I said I want her to search me."

"Why, so you can have some woman playing with your balls?"

He gaped at me.

"I said pull your pants up. I can't stand here all day."

When he didn't obey my order, I pulled up his pants and stuck my hands down between his thigh and grabbed his balls. "Yep, nothing much here."

Everyone started laughing, inmates and guards alike. The inmate started complaining about mistreatment. I told him to get inside the block. It was a bluff, talking tough, but it worked. I had passed my first test … and all because of lessons learned as a thirteen-year old boy in North Beach.

Finally, I finished my first shift and was able to leave. When I got into my car, I slumped against the seat. I felt as though I had been in a war zone and survived. When I got home, Amy was waiting, about as nervous as I had been that first moment in the South Yard.

"How did it go?" she asked.

Taking the Rudy-club I had been told to keep in my wall locker, I swung it through the air, again and again, as though striking someone to the ground. "Get back in the cell, you son of a bitch," I yelled, forgetting I had left San Quentin.

Amy recoiled in horror. "I knew it. I knew you would change and become an animal like them."

"Honey, I'm only kidding. Believe me."

From the look in her eyes she didn't.

In the first few weeks, I think I caught on quicker than the other guards who had started with me. Maybe knowing how to react around the inmates came from being with my father. Not only could I spot the predictable, but the unpredictable as well.

Amy quit asking me about my job, and I stopped telling her.

She hated what I was doing, and I hated not being able to tell her all the things that had happened or what I had learned.

As for my father, it was as though by becoming a correctional officer, I had betrayed him and his world. We stopped communicating for a while, which was fine with me. I started having a few drinks after work at a bar frequented by other correctional officers. We had our own clique at a booth in the corner. We'd sit there drinking, badmouthing inmates who had given us grief and putting down officers that we didn't trust. If there was an initiation for new guards, I didn't have to go through it, or maybe I had without knowing it. But I quickly became one of the guys, just the way I had with my father's friends.

Hanging around after work with the other officers was like being with my father's buddies at Roland's. In fact, it surprised me how much correctional officers acted like the connected guys in San Francisco. The only thing that made them different was the uniform. Aside from that, they could have been the same group of people. And for both, the one quality that was necessary above all: loyalty.

Guards never talked about their work to strangers, an officer told me one night. "The inmates write all the fuckin' books. We're like the walls. We don't speak. We keep everything to ourselves."

Within two months, I had worked in the kitchen and the hospital, I had been on all the different blocks, and even in the prison within the prison, the Adjustment Center. Although it would have been crazy to say I felt at home, I was starting to find my way through what I heard an inmate describe as "a labyrinth with no way out, only in." Maybe for him; not for me. I got to go home every night. His home was his cell.

I took whatever job I was given without complaint. My attitude must have been noticed by the sergeants, who then told the lieutenants, and they told the captains. I was offered my first overtime shift, which I gladly accepted. Sixteen hours, I reasoned, was like getting a double salary.

When I got home the next morning, Amy was scared to death. She thought something bad had happened to me and had called the prison. But they wouldn't pass the call through while I was inside. All they did was tell her that I was working.

I told her that I had doubled my salary. If I could get a few days of overtime a month, we could start buying the things we had dreamed about owning.

She looked hurt.

I was angry. Having no money for so long and now having the chance to earn more than I had ever made legally, I wondered why she couldn't support me. I got a couple hours of sleep and then went to unwind with my buddies before going back on my regular shift. That's when I got my first real dose of San Quentin violence, "up close and personal," as they say now. All during the first few months working at San Quentin, nothing serious had happened. A few homemade stills had been busted up, and two homemade knives were found buried in the South Yard, but nothing serious had occurred—yet.

I was inside South Block, getting ready to check on the inmates in the shower area. I went upstairs and walked inside the large tiled room, where seven or eight inmates were toweling off against the wall.

As soon as I walked in, some inmates started rushing out the door. "You guys are real fast," I said. "You know when it's time to go."

I spotted another group of five or six near the showers by themselves. Then I noticed a man lying motionless in one of the shower stalls, with a pool of red formed around him—what officials would describe in a press release as "liquid later identified as blood." I looked to the right and saw a large object in one of the urinals. It resembled a discarded wig. As I walked closer, it appeared someone had stuck a cat in the urinal. But it wasn't moving. I'm looking at this thing, and I'm starting to realize what I'm looking at ... a decapitated head.

I was so stunned I couldn't move. Finally, one of the inmates came up behind me. "Blow the whistle," he exclaimed.

I didn't respond.

He leaned closer. "Blow the whistle, man, or you're gonna get killed."

For a second, my mouth was too dry to blow the whistle, but I found enough moisture to make it work. That whistle was so loud I'm sure the warden heard it in his office. I had blown it during training at the Academy. But it was outdoors, and I only put a little force into it. Now I blew with all my might and my ears rang for seconds from the piercing sound.

Every inmate still in the shower tore past me, racing to get away before help arrived. Within seconds, six guards had rushed in beside me. "What happened?" the lieutenant asked.

"Uh, I think there's a guy's head in the urinal," I managed to say.

Minutes later, the investigators showed up. "Can you identify who you saw in here when you found the body?" one asked.

I was so petrified from seeing the head in the urinal that I couldn't recall the inmates in the shower—whether they were white, black, or brown. All I could remember was seeing the body in the shower and the head several feet away.

One of the officers grabbed the head by its black hair and lifted it high in the air. Turning it around toward us, the sergeant took the dead man's jaw and began opening and closing it, like a ventriloquist with a dummy. "I've been having a real bad day," lisped the officer. "Everyone's been pissing on me."

Every officer started laughing—everyone but me. I was still thinking about what the inmate had said into my ear: "Blow that whistle, man, or you're gonna get killed."

I reached up to make sure the whistle was still pinned to my shirt. It had saved my life. I'd never let it out of reach. That night I tried to tell Amy what had happened, but she didn't want to hear about it. She didn't want to hear about anything that took place inside the walls. "But that's where I work. That's gonna be half my life," I said angrily.

"Not the half with me," she said, walking out of the room.

Moments later I left. I needed to go where I could talk about the head in the urinal. I knew that if I didn't leave the job somewhere between San Quentin and home, my job was going to start coming home with me. And I knew Amy wasn't ready for that.

Time went quickly, especially with more and more overtime. I could have it almost anytime I wanted it—for I never turned down the bad jobs and so I got the good ones, too. I worked in the laundry, along the gun rails, in the Visiting Room, in the factory area, with transportation, in the barber shop, in the medical section, in the dental section, and in each of the four blocks—North, South, East, and West. I worked Death Row and the Adjustment Center. I worked gun tiers and towers. I got to be like the brooms in <u>Fantasia</u>, working faster and faster, more and more. I was young and strong and getting hooked on the adrenaline that started rushing through me the moment I walked through the first set of sliding metal doors. "This is it," I would tell myself, "where they separate the men from the boys." No time-out here. This is the tightrope over the abyss, and I loved walking it, because I knew that no matter what—I would never fall.

I had crossed my childhood without losing my balance. San Quentin was like multiple versions of my father all squeezed into different cells.

I was a quick learner. Having been a bag boy taught me how to read inmates the same way I had read people in North Beach. The rules for getting killed were simple: snitching on someone who had broken the rules; rolling over to get out of a gang and telling on everyone; or a bad drug deal, a bad business deal; or even for refusing to use your wife and kids as mules to bring in drugs. Retribution didn't stop at the gate either. If you did roll over and were moved into isolation to protect you, someone from the gang would be waiting when you got out, and you'd be just as dead. Someone on the outside would order an inmate to be killed within the walls, and he'd be taken out. The reasons for getting killed were as numerous as the ways to get killed. Guards were a little further back from the fray. For an officer to get murdered, permission would have to be granted by the gang leaders. That doesn't mean an inmate couldn't explode and choke out an officer before a gunman could come down the railing and get a clear shot at him.

But officers had a sort of yellow square around them, and an inmate knew that if he moved inside it, he could be shot. The officer, too, knew if an inmate came over that invisible line between them, that he didn't give a shit—that he was ready to die to kill him.

So I watched, I listened, and most of all I let inmates know that I was neither a sadist who liked fucking with them for the sake of it, nor a coward who would back down when trouble started. I had to walk a narrow path ... about as wide as the twin tiers that rose five levels—with the gaping hole separating the two sides covered with mesh to keep inmates and prisoners from being hurled over the railing. Two facing sets of approximately seventy-five cells where inmates and guards were separated by no more than a few feet—no greater distance than the length of a spear. Behind a metal screen on a railing isolated from the tiers was a gunman, clutching a rifle or, in Death Row, a pistol. The gunman moved ahead of each guard on the tier, making certain no one was lying in wait. But if he wasn't paying attention, was hung over or worried about debts—or even carrying a grudge against the officer on the tier—he might not react in time to save the guard on the tier.

I had to beat the same horrible truth into my head time after time: Ain't nobody here I can count on but me. And sometimes I couldn't even count on me.

Violence in prison is like a fever that can never be eradicated but only kept from raging out of control ... not by medicine, but by force.

That fever can become contagious. I saw officers change from the day they came in, go from being decent human beings to brutes who took pleasure in aggravating the prisoners. I came to see that each of the guards had a kind of red circle over his chest that only the inmates could see. If he was fair with them, the red was faint; if he was cruel or unjust, it was bold red. Sooner or later, his pay-back would come. The inmates never forget a slight or an insult. They had 24 hours a day to memorize it over and over again until it was embedded in their minds and they thought of nothing else.

Once I passed my period of probation, I got a raise and started accepting more and more overtime. I was transferred up to Death Row, on the sixth floor of the North Block, Death Row is an independent unit, with its own rules and larger cells for the condemned men, who are kept one to a cell. One of the differences about working on Death Row is that you have to get to know the inmates. Those men up there know the only way they're getting out, unless a miracle occurs and they are pardoned because of DNA proving they aren't guilty of the murder they were sentenced for, is to kill a guard and get another trial. Killing an inmate won't get a man off of Death Row, but killing a guard will. There will have to be a new trial and a whole new criminal process; and the killer will know that for a period of time his death sentence will be postponed, even if he will be con-demned for the murder of the staff member and sent back to Death Row to be executed. He'll have gotten a reprieve, even if only for a few months, long enough to be taken outside the walls under heavy escort to see, however briefly from inside a speeding van on the way to court, what life looks like beyond the walls.

Usually, though, condemned inmates are quiet and don't cause any trouble. There are occasional fights or stabbings, but they are usually directed against inmates, not against the guards. The men on Death Row don't have time to waste. They can hear the clock ticking inside their heads. And most of them are focused on working on their legal documents, trying to find something, any-thing, that will grant them a stay of execution.

When I worked Death Row, I played chess with Charles Manson, who, when the cameras weren't on him, was as normal as any psychopath can be. He didn't rant or rave or even say weird things on the block. But let a reporter show up to interview him, and Satan would emerge.

The only true figures of evil I encountered were both multiple killers.

Lyle Banks had murdered two teenage brothers, and afterward he ate the ham-burgers they had been enjoying the moment before he approached them. It would have been bad enough, killing a couple of kids for no reason—but then Banks started bragging about it during exercise in the enclosed yard reserved for inmates on Death Row.

Inmates soon got tired of hearing Banks go on about killing the kids in cold blood, so one night six guys raped him in the showers. And they took their time inflicting as much pain as they could on Banks. It was payback for the two boys.

What Banks was really known for, though, was how much contraband he could store up his rectum. UPS couldn't get as much packed in one of their trucks as Banks could up his rectum—everything from hacksaw blades to buck knives, and all at the same time. Once, guards X-rayed Banks and discovered twelve full-sized hacksaw blades, about thirty smaller hacksaw blades, and two buck knives concealed inside him. He even had syringes and razor blades up his rectum. All had been sealed with melted wax to keep him from cutting himself. The weapons turned up during an x-ray of Banks's abdomen. Everyone wanted to know how he had got the weapons in the first place. I thought they had been given to him in the hospital after the beating he got while being raped. Some people said Banks had paid a guard to smuggle in the blades, but I didn't believe it. In all the time I was at San Quentin only two guards were fired for bringing contraband into the prison.

The night before he died, Banks ordered enough food for a football team, but, hey, I figured, let him eat what he wants. He'd be going on a long diet after that. He had pizza, steak, cheeseburgers, chocolate cake, jelly beans, French fries, Coca-Cola, and milkshakes.

After his execution, no one missed him.

The sickest individual I encountered up on the sixth floor was Burt Chambers: a Marin County man who had kidnapped several young women and while torturing them to death in his van recorded their screams, pleas, and moaning. He petitioned to have his tapes as evidence for his appeal. Against his own feelings and judgment, the warden was forced to let Chambers have his monstrous device. At night, just when every one was starting to get to sleep … a woman would begin sobbing and then screaming as I never heard before and have never heard since. We'd run down to Chambers's cell, where we'd find him masturbating while listening to himself tear out a victim's fingernails or yank her nipples off with pliers. We'd confiscate the tapes until his attorney petitioned to have them returned. But the damage would have been done. Most of the other inmates would find nightmares surging up in their sleep…. all because of Chambers.

Finally, his last appeal was rejected and Chambers was gassed. When the bell started pealing the first of the thirteen gongs, many inmates and more than a few officers shouted out their approval. One less monster stalking the earth.

As I finished my shift one afternoon on Death Row, I got a phone call to report to the execution chamber. I knew that no execution was scheduled so I wasn't worried I was going to have to escort someone to the gas chamber. I found three sergeants standing around the pale green cylinder containing two metal chairs.

It was eerie, the thick glass, and the chairs with holes in them so the gas can reach the condemned person's lungs more quickly. One of the officers said they merely needed to check the curtains on the windows and needed me to go sit inside.

I walked in and took a seat on one of the cold chairs. The officers swung the massive, airtight door closed and swung the handles sealing the chamber. Even though I knew nothing was going to happen, I felt scared and more alone than I could ever remember. Suddenly there was a clank, and a loud hissing began. The curtains slid shut. I bolted out of my seat and ran up to the window, pounding on the thick glass. "Quit fucking around!," I yelled. "Let me out of here!"

The hissing didn't stop. I stopped, sniffing the air, thinking maybe some freak accident had occurred and cyanide had been released. A moment later, the handle spun around, and the door swung open. "Thanks, Woolf," one of the officers said. "Everything seems to be working. That was just the air vent you heard."

"Fuck you, guys. You come in here and sit down."

Soon I was laughing, but walking out of the room I did glance back at that strange object resembling a diving bell. I never have seen a place so lonely, before or since.

-#-

7

Walled Up

I quickly learned that a maximum security prison is a different country where your ID is your passport. Dangerous, too, even though every inch has been mapped, searched, and controlled—because at any moment you can get killed by any of the people living in that landscape of steel, concrete, and stone. Like cadavers, maximum security prison blocks possess a smell that, once experienced, is never forgotten. Hard to describe—a mixture of stale air, unwashed bodies, burning paper, and smoldering meat.

There are a few basic rules for surviving there. One, keep your eyes open. Two, take nothing for granted, absolutely nothing. The inmates have their own language, and their own system of justice and retribution, completely different from your own. I tried to learn to interpret everything—even the different forms of silence, and what they might mean. Maybe if I learned the codes inside the walls, I might make it back from that foreign county, night after night, day after day, year after year. Inside that world, everything is a sign of something else. Nothing just <u>is</u>. It always refers to something else. All the mail going out, all the mail coming in, I soon discovered, contains messages not only in terms of the words being used, but concealed within terms of salutation or an endearment. Even the way the stamps are placed on the envelopes means something to someone else. And this territory belongs to the enemy. It may look peaceful, but it could erupt at any moment. I had to recognize the codes—even something as insignificant as the position of a pillow on a bed, or the way a book was left open on a shelf. All meant something to someone else—and I tried to make certain that someone else was me.

Paranoia in prison is not paranoia. It is necessary for survival.

There are more languages in prison than in all the dictionaries in the world. And if you don't speak them, rarely will anyone want to teach you. You have to learn them alone, word by word, meaning by meaning. And when the inmates sense you've mastered one language, they'll discard it and take up another.

It's a hopeless task to stay up with a swirl of communication that doesn't make a sound.... but you must try to understand, for even a different form of silence on the tiers might be signaling your death warrant.

No one who hasn't been inside a maximum security prison, whether officer or inmate, knows what it is like when the gates clang shut behind you. The fear is something that can't be imagined, a form of multiple claustrophobia pressing down on you from all sides. I never got used to it, never. And if I started to think that everything might be okay, there would be the greeting I received every single time I went in to begin work. "Woolf, just to let you know, nothing has changed from the day before. We have a no-hostage policy." It was a reminder that when it came down to sacrificing me to keep prisoners from escaping, there wouldn't even be a moment's hesitation. I was a dead man.

Such awareness of your own professional vulnerability makes officers always try to stay in view of other officers. You try to avoid moving out of eyesight, because then you are alone and at the mercy of the inmates. You accept that for every gunman watching you from a tier, there are twenty inmates staring at you from inside cells.

You have to always to remind yourself to be aware. The one time you let your guard down (no pun intended) is when you will be stabbed or shot, simply because that's the moment you are most vulnerable. I learned always to know who was behind me, in front of me, next to me, even on a tier above me. In prison you have to realize you can only count on yourself. You can't depend on other correctional officers, even if you've been told you can.

It's like coming up on a group of inmates. You never want to just walk up on them without a sound. You want them to know you are coming, so they can quit talking about killing someone who rolled over on them … until you pass. I used to keep my keys hooked to the front of my trousers, so wherever I walked I made a jingling noise, letting them know I was coming.

To remind the guards never to take their safety for granted, there was the death of Sergeant Wentworth. The rumor was that he was set up for "pay back." The truth is, any incident, no matter how small, might have led to Sergeant Wentworth's death. I had heard it was "payback." Yet because of all the ties, connections, intrigues, insults, and injuries, let alone free-floating rage and madness in prison, I don't know if "payback" was the true reason behind's Wentworth's death. Who knows why he said he wanted to see a sergeant and stood waiting in the darkness of his cell for Wentworth to come down the tier. It could have been any correctional officer; it didn't matter who appeared. Wentworth forgot something that every correctional officer is trained to always remember: Never enter a darkened area alone. He paid for the mistake with his life.

Wentworth was speared by a homemade spear, thrust out of a cell at night on a darkened tier where he had no business being. Sergeants direct other staff. They never go on the tiers unless they are requested by a counselor or by upper echelon staff. Sergeants don't do "the count," the guards do.

If an inmate says, I want to see sergeant so-and-so, then the sergeant will go up—but never by himself, especially when an overhead light is burned out.

Even though there is a gunman inside an enclosed railing, he can't always see well enough to protect any guard passing by the cells. Unless a skull and cross-bones had been painted on the wall of the block, saying, "Sergeant Wentworth, you're gonna die tonight," you can't get any more warning signs than the ones he saw: darkened tier, being alone, night.

The gunman should have warned the sergeant off the tier—but he was new, so he said nothing, merely walking a few cells ahead of the sergeant, several feet away on the tier, certain that no inmate was waiting up against his cell door.

But the gunman couldn't see because of the darkness.

In an instant, the spear came thrusting out and hit Wentworth in the sternum, splitting it open. He grunted once, clutched his chest, and turned to go for help. Then he collapsed.

It stunned the staff. A good man had been killed in the time it took to blow out a match. The man who killed the sergeant didn't care that he was gonna be tried for murder and end up on Death Row. If it was payback, he was carrying out orders from his buddies. If he hadn't speared the sergeant, he would have been stabbed himself.

I never learned the real reason behind the sergeant's death. But one thing I knew: If the inmates want to take you out, they'll take you out.

Prison retaliation is like a few drops of water running out of a mountain peak, heading downhill, melting and joining other drops of water to form a stream, which, as it continues downward, becomes wider, stronger, deeper. Before you know it there's a raging river breaking through canyons, heading toward the sea. That's how payback works in prison, except the drops don't contain water. They're acid filled with hate.

A few weeks after Wentworth's death, an Hispanic inmate got his cell door open as another officer and I were escorting a handcuffed black inmate. We had no sooner gotten the black inmate into his cell when the Mexican inmate ran in and began stabbing him. We leaped on him as quickly as we could, but his arm was pumping back and forth like a piston. In the time it took us to react, the Mexican had stabbed the black inmate thirty-two times.

The inmate must have had his guardian angel hovering real close, because he survived. We got him down to the hospital in time for the doctors to staunch the bleeding and get transfusions of blood into him. You think he might have been grateful that we had wasted no time getting him downstairs. But no: He thought that we purposefully let the Mexican loose to get in and kill him. Once he started talking to his "homies," those little drops of hate started moving in our direction.

As an old-timer told me before retiring, "A maximum security prison is not a place to rehabilitate men and women who have made a mistake and are atoning for their crime by serving time. A maximum security prison is a modern fortress meant to keep monsters from breaking out and ravaging the surrounding countryside."

I thought he was exaggerating. I came to realize that he telling the truth. Every time I came in the gate, I knew that I was entering a world of seven thousand men, have of whom were "max," who had forfeited their freedom for whatever they had done. Even if 90 percent of them were, as they said, innocent, there were still 10 percent who were guilty. And for those doing life without parole, they had nothing to lose because they had nothing to gain. Yet I tried to treat every one of them with respect. Officers are told never to ask an inmate what crime he was sent up for. Once he knows, then that officer is going to treat that inmate differently, be it better, say, for an extortionist, and worse, for a pedophile. So you don't ask. You treat each inmate alike until he does something that makes you treat him differently.

I tried always to make sure they had hot food and that their mail got to them. They may have lost all their rights as citizens, but they hadn't lost their rights as human beings to me. It is the way I would have wanted to be treated were I on the other side of the bars.

A lot of officers did just the opposite. They went out of their way to remind the inmates they were prisoners—not giving them clean linen and handing them their dinner saying, "Here's your food. If you don't like it, fuck you. That's all you get."

You still had to be careful when saying "yes" to an inmate, like when an inmate wanted to swap his pudding for another inmate's bread and fresh fruit. You had to remember bread and fruit, along with sugar, were used to make wine.

One of the hardest things at San Quentin, for me, was seeing the really old inmates who would never get out alive. They've got no family, so nobody writes to them, and they're too old to be in the gangs. So they were just waiting to die.

Many times, though, inmates who have been in San Quentin for thirty or forty years and haven't had any confrontations with officers or any infraction slips in their record jackets will be moved into the library or given a cushy job.

When it was quiet at night and I would be doing overtime up in one of the towers, I used to look down at the enormous complex of buildings, never dark but always illuminated like an airport runway, so that everything could be seen. But I knew there was another kind of darkness that couldn't be permeated by all the light in the world.

It was the accumulated darkness of all of the prisoners who had lived and died there, for San Quentin had been a prison since before Abraham Lincoln was president. I used to get bored on the tower and try to imagine how many men and women—for women used to be sent to San Quentin—had been sentenced there since the first wall went up.

One night, I played a stupid game by pretending that each prisoner had spent an average of ten years, then combined the number of years of all the prisoners who had ever been sentenced to the prison. I finally gave up. Even though I don't give any credence to one of Amy's girlfriends talking about Feng Shui, and how spaces can influence how people feel, I know that the soil of San Quentin has absorbed so much despair that it's a miracle that flowers grow inside the walls.

-#-

8

Time Out

Inmates hone to an art what's going on and "what's going down" around them. They watch you better than you can them—because they have "all day," or all the time on their side, which means years to "get over on" (fool, trick, or win over) the guards Whether it's alive or dead makes little difference to many of them. I knew inmates who would stab someone in the yard to get to go to court, and I knew inmates who completed a ten-year sentence and committed a felony the day they were released in order to be sent back to San Quentin.

Their reasoning was: It's better to be something small inside the walls than nothing outside them.

No matter how well you thought you knew an inmate, you always had to remind yourself where he was and where you were. As with the moon, you had to remember that there was a hidden side you couldn't see … that could come out at any time, as it did to Wendy.

Wendy was a sergeant on the security squad in a secured housing unit. A good capable officer, with years of experience, she represented all that was best about the old school: confident, fair, and smart. She knew her way around San Quentin.

One day, about a year after I started, she had been assigned to interrogate a member of the Mexican gang in an office on the main floor of the Adjustment Center, the area where the prison's most dangerous inmates were kept isolated. She knew this inmate; so did I. He was a hardened felon who had been in for years. While serving time, he had assaulted another inmate, and that's when I first came to know him—escorting him to court.

Montoya knew he was in for life and would never be getting out of prison—but he didn't hassle the guards. He and I had never had any problems together; at least he hadn't caused me any trouble before. It was Montoya's dealings with other members of his gang and hassles with other officers that kept him isolated in the Adjustment Center.

But finally he was getting ready to be returned to Maintenance Housing, a lower level of security in the West Block. As soon as he had learned he was being moved to a new cell, he requested seeing a counselor. Wendy was assigned to see him. Although she had been on the security squad for years, she had decided to move up in rank and become a counselor.

With her experience and qualifications, she easily made the transition. No longer monitoring inmates, she started combining the roles of both psychologist and sociologist: trying to learn about gang members and what was going on behind the scenes with the inmates, and helping to maintain the fragile truce on which a maximum security prison is always precariously balanced. Being a counselor is a position that requires a great deal of insight and intelligence. Wendy had both. She was good at her job, respected by most inmates and officers alike. This is not an easy thing to accomplish, for rarely do both groups respect the same guard. Wendy, though, knew how to deal with inmates, and they could tell she was fair. In fact, Wendy was the same officer who had escorted me out of the Administration Building following my second interview to be hired as a correctional officer, and she was the person who said, "Ask me no questions, I'll tell you no lies," when I asked if I was going to be hired. And here we were, working the same shift, although in different parts of the prison.

An officer went up to the Adjustment Center to bring Montoya down to the counselor's office to talk with Wendy. As other inmates are being escorted around the area, it is important that an inmate knows no other inmate can see him being interviewed. The rumor might start that he was giving up information. So the curtains were always kept closed to protect the identity of the inmate inside. The glass, too, is extra thick to prevent inmates from hearing what is being said inside The only person who can hear and see what goes on is the escort officer whose job is to stand outside the door, watching the counselor and inmate in the office and making sure that everything is under control.

Everything went as planned. Montoya came in and sat down at the table, and Wendy started talking to him. Then for some reason, which was never explained, the escort officer left the viewing window—something he is never supposed to do. I heard a scuffle had broken out down the hall and he went to quell it—but whatever the cause, that left Montoya alone with Wendy ... just for a moment. That's all it took for Montoya to look up and see no one watching him. He was alone with a woman. With one punch, he knocked her to the floor. An instant later, he was tearing off her pants.

By the time the escort officer returned, Wendy had been savagely raped. Four officers grabbed Montoya and pulled him away from Wendy. Two others tended to Wendy.

I heard what had happened after I finished the count in North Block. I couldn't believe the cynicism of a couple of the officers. They said that Wendy got what she deserved, that she had probably been screwing Montoya when the escort officer came back and found them. And, they added, she had probably torn her clothes off to fake being raped. It was brutal, both the rape and what was being said by a few officers. Even though generally respected and liked, Wendy had made enemies being a counselor, for not only did counselors investigate gang activity, but they also checked that gangs weren't on the take with guards.

Their total lack of feelings shocked me. It was only two or three correctional officers, but that was enough.

Montoya was returned to the Adjustment Center after first being taken to the hospital to be treated for injuries suffered when he "slipped and fell" on the floor. When he was brought in, Wendy was being given emergency treatment before being transferred to Marin General Hospital.

Within the next few hours, everyone in the prison knew what had happened to Wendy in the Adjustment Center and who was responsible. The inmates were so disgusted with Montoya that some came up with a plan to kill him the following morning. Through his gang members in the Adjustment Center, Montoya got wind of the plot to murder him. Late that night, he tore off part of his pillow case and wrapped it around his neck, holding his head about an inch and a half above his the pillow. He then wrapped the other end of the strip around the heating vent. As he started to doze off and go to sleep, his head began putting more and more pressure around his windpipe.

In the morning, he didn't respond to the count. The extraction team was called to go in and get him. It's against the rules for one officer to go in and try to rouse an unresponsive inmate. He could have been feigning, concealing a homemade weapon under his pillow. But Montoya wasn't breathing. Basically, he had hanged himself while going to sleep.

As officers moved his body out of the cell, inmates start pelting Montoya's corpse with cups of urine and wads of excrement. Of course, it splattered onto the guards, too, but it wasn't meant for them. It was directed at Montoya. For them, he had done a chicken-shit thing by raping an officer, and one they respected. To increase their contempt, he had committed suicide ... before they could kill him.

What had happened wasn't simply between Montoya and Wendy. Once Montoya raped that guard, the repercussions spread through every block. The inmates knew that there would be "payback" against all of them for what one of them had done.

Montoya's brutal act brought heat down on his gang, on the people in the Adjustment Center, and on the West Block. Of course, the one who would be scarred for life was Wendy. But her character and strength carried her through her recovery. After being raped by an inmate, ninety-nine of a hundred other guards, male or female, would have transferred out of the prison or quit, never to return to San Quentin. Wendy stayed. In fact, she later became associate warden.

Aside from the attack taking place at all, the biggest surprise was learning who had done it. Yes, Montoya was in a gang, and yes, he had been convicted of aggravated assault against another inmate; but Montoya and I had built up a little sense of reciprocal trust. I thought I knew him. From escorting him through blocks, I had come to sense that he didn't want to cause trouble. Sure, he had his deals with his "homies," but he didn't want to stir up trouble with the officers. Or so I thought. It hurt not only for what happened to Wendy, but for my failure to see the other side of Montoya.

Weeks before, he had come up to me when I was searching his cell, and he slipped a "kite" into the uneaten food on his plate. I spotted the note and opened it when I got off the tier. "Down" was the only word in the note. Knowing what he meant, I cuffed him and brought him down to the sergeant's office. When we got down there, he started telling us a group of the Mexicans and the blacks had plans to get the staff.

Sergeant Finley said he needed more information.

Montoya smiled. "You know, something there's something I seen on TV that I'd like. I've never had a McDonald's hamburger."

Finley turned to me. "Woolf, why don't you do a lunch-run and get Montoya a McDonald's cheeseburger and fries."

There I was, twenty minutes later, driving down to Larkspur to buy a Big Mac with fries. Later, the sergeant got the food into Montoya's cell without anyone else seeing what he was taking in.

The next day he and I used the pretext of "tossing" Montoya's cell to ask him what he knew. Montoya kept his word. "Be ready tomorrow," he whispered, "when you go down to the yard." Montoya told us that the blacks and Mexicans were pissed at the white inmates and were going to get them and the white officers, too.

We left the cell and reported the plan to the captain.

Apparently, the inmates involved thought they would have a better chance of success in the yard than they would while being escorted down the stairs from the tiers.

Unlike the South Yard, where as many as two thousand inmates circulate freely, except near the dead line, the Adjustment Center has three separate yards each divided by high chain fences: The whites are on the far side, the blacks in the center, and the Hispanics on the other side. When you take them food, you count how many inmates are in each separated section, then you call one inmate from one group at a time to step inside the gate between the yard and the cell-block. You give that one inmate lunches for however many people are in his group.

It came out that while I was handing out lunches to the whites, the black inmates planned to scale the fence, take me hostage, and try to force the guards to open the door. Sergeant Finley told me everything he had learned from another note that Montoya had sent him in his uneaten breakfast.

"Woolf, do you have a problem with running back inside the unit once you hear the gunman rack his shotgun? If you don't wanna go out there, I understand. But if we change the routine, the inmates are gonna know that Montoya talked, and we're gonna have a whole new set of problems."

I said I'd do it, but I wanted to know one thing: Who was going to be watching me? Sergeant Finley said two officers would be sent up to the roof of North Block with high-powered rifles equipped with laser-scopes. They would be covering every step I made. If any of the inmates started coming to the gate, let alone trying to scale it, the officers were going to start firing.

There had to be at least forty black inmates in the center yard and thirty Hispanics to their right. I figured if they all took off for the fence, one or two of them would make it over the top and get to me. What worried me most, though, were all the bullets coming down from the roof. I knew that no matter how good a shot the snipers were, there would be total confusion at the fence.

But I wasn't going to turn back, and to use prison jargon for someone who gives in to fear, "pee all over myself." So I took the lunches and opened the door. I motioned to one of the inmates to pick up the lunches. As I was handing him sandwiches, I made out a movement in the middle section. Guys were starting to press together against the wall as though they were getting ready to go for the fence. Everything seemed poised on the edge of a moment. One false move and everything would come down on me.

I was trying not to show any fear, but I could feel the adrenaline rushing, and I knew that two rifles were already aimed right at us. I kept thinking, "Shit, can I get back to the door if bullets are hitting around me?" I had at least thirty feet to run to reach the door and the inmates had half that distance. It didn't look good. I decided that once the gunfire started, I was going to drop to the ground and hide behind the gate control panel.

I trusted the snipers. They were old-school riflemen. They had shot inmates before, but I knew they had also shot staff who got in the way. Of course, they preferred not to hit the wrong people, but when it came down to letting a prisoner get loose, it didn't matter who went down. Nobody was escaping.

I finished handing out lunch to the whites and motioned for one of the black inmates to come get the lunches for his group. All this time, the Mexicans were pushing their hands against the wall as though getting ready to run for the fence.

The black inmates stepped in and I shut the gate. One inmate looked down at the sandwiches and then glanced up at the roof where the snipers were lying in prone position.

"What's up, Woolf?"

"What do you mean, 'What's up?'" I said, playing dumb.

"What are those dudes doin' up there?"

"Shit, they're here to make sure I don't have complaints about the lunch."

"Come on, quit the shuck and jive."

I looked the guy right in the eyes. "Shit, man, you guys would do better hunting bears with a switch than fuck with this little white guy."

The inmate started laughing. Minutes later, he's back talking with his people, and the blacks see that something's up … then they spot the snipers, too. Now everybody's confused. Someone in the Mexican group yelled, "Fuck you, pussies. Kill that white guard."

But the threat was over; I could feel it. The stance had softened within the two groups. Like wild animals abandoning their prey, they began breaking off into ones and twos and eating their sandwiches. I stepped back inside the block and slid to the floor, exhausted. I felt as though I had been holding my breath for minutes.

Half a dozen officers turned from the windows where they had been watching.

"You okay, Woolf?" one asked.

"No, I'm dead. What do you think?"

Officers started trading money, and I realized that they had been betting on whether I would make it. Sergeant Finley made fifty bucks. I would have been worried if he had lost.

Even though I was out of breath, I knew that I was still breathing because of Montoya. Without the information he had given us, I might have been taken hostage, and from there it would only have been a matter of time before I would have been stabbed to death or mistakenly shot. All for a Big Mac and fries.

Every time I thought of what he had done for me it was cancelled out by what he had done to Wendy. Nothing was left. A blank O with a face painted over it. Who was Montoya? Which Montoya was the real one, the rapist or the guy who saved my life? Montoya was dead. I'd never learn the answer—not that there was one. It was then that I realized I could never know an inmate. I could only watch what he was doing and try to keep him from doing things that would hurt others.

They were worse than wild animals. With animals, you can tell when they are cornered, hungry, wounded, protecting their young ... but with inmates you could never tell when a smile would conceal a snarl, or a cupped hand conceal a shaved-down razor blade. Some people think that wild animals attack without provocation. They rarely do. There is always something that sets them off, some-thing that leads directly back to their behavior: a hiker walking along with an unwrapped chicken sandwich in his pack and being mauled by a cougar, or a woman camping in the wilderness during her menstrual period and being attacked by a bear. They send out signals that they are prey and the predators respond.

The cliché about prison being a jungle isn't true. A prison is much more dan-gerous. A water hole in the middle of the yard where inmates from all the gangs would gather to kneel down and drink water together? Impossible. It'd be undrinkable from all the blood spilled before the first sunset ended.

To let off the accumulating stress, I started spending more and more time in bars, either in Marin County or in San Francisco. One night I met a dancer in the Tenderloin who told me she had become a stripper to earn money to get through graduate school. She wanted to be a psychologist. We had a few drinks and she started asking me those questions people do when they meet someone they'll probably never see again—the kind you ask to get to know someone as quick as you can because you're going to forget them just as fast.

When she asked what I did, I told her I was in law enforcement. I didn't want to scare her away by saying I worked at a maximum security prison. People carry around a lot of baggage when it comes to meeting a correctional officer. Either they have a relative who did time, or they've read about a scandal involving guards brutalizing inmates, or they hate capital punishment and hold all guards responsible for being killers. Saying you're a prison guard isn't the same as saying, "I'm in sales."

When she asked me what branch of law enforcement I was in, I lied and said, "Juvenile Hall."

"Oh, the one out past Twin Peaks?"

"The same."

"Oh, I go by there to see my aunt. It looks like such a sad place."

"There are worse places, believe me."

"But they have barbed wire fences."

"Those kids are there for a reason."

"But they're so young."

"Hey, San Quentin's got inmates sixteen years old."

She seemed shocked by my remark. "I thought San Quentin was only for adults."

"Are you serious? Some so-called minors have killed four or five people in "their hood" and maybe even a cop. You think Preston or Tracy can keep them under control?"

"I'm sorry, Preston and what?"

"CYA, California Youth Authority, last stop before adult prison. The more violent felons go right to maximum prison. And if they, excuse my English, fuck up, they go to San Quentin."

"At sixteen?"

"At sixteen."

"That's terrible. They've probably all had a bad childhood."

I took a swig of my drink. "A lot of people have had a bad childhood, but they don't all become killers or rapists."

"I suppose not, but at sixteen you can still change."

"Like cement, huh?"

"What do you mean?"

"Well, when it's still soft, you can shape it—but as it hardens, it becomes more and more difficult to work with. Then it sets, and the only thing you can do is break it apart."

"Like walls?" she asked.

"I guess," I answered, not sure if she was trying to make a point.

She had to go and perform, but later she came back and we went to another spot to drink. She was strange. I wasn't used to being with a woman who's a stripper, which meant one thing to me, and then talking in such an intellectual way about everything, which meant something else. I just wanted to have a few laughs before going home and continuing my unbroken argument with Amy about why I was coming home so late every night. But the dancer was starting to bother me. When we stopped at the North Star for a drink, I started to figure how to get rid of her so I could go. She just talked too much, and the more silent

I was, the more she thought it was a challenge, like I was a mystery she was going to solve. Out of nowhere, the woman told me to close my eyes. I thought maybe she wanted to kiss me or run some number on me. But I did as she said.

"Imagine you are in a forest at night and it's foggy," she said. "Suddenly you see a high wall in front of you. Do you see it?"

"What are you talking about?"

"It's just a test. Try pretending to see what I'm describing. Can you see the wall?"

I concentrated for a few moments. Finally, I did see something that looked like a wall. "Yeah, yeah, I see it."

"Good, now see the opening in the side, not a door, but an opening large enough for you to get through. Do you see it?"

It was easier this time. "Yeah."

"Go through the wall."

"Okay, I'm going through," I said, half-going-along with her and half-wanting to see what would come next.

"Beyond the wall, you see many men in the same grey clothing, standing in line, but they aren't moving, just shifting from foot to foot in place. Do you see them?"

"Yes, some of them are even looking at me."

"Good. Now where are you?"

"What?"

"Are you in the line or next to it?"

"Uh…. I'm in the line."

She paused. "Wrong answer."

I opened my eyes. "What do you mean?"

"It's a perception test of seeing and being seen, passive and active perception."

"I don't get it."

"It just means you perceive yourself part of a group without seeing yourself separate from it."

I must have looked upset, for she leaned over.

"What's wrong?"

"Nothing. I was just thinking, I shouldn't have answered the way I did."

"Why not?"

"Because I'm really a guard at San Quentin, and your test made me sound like a prisoner."

She looked startled for a moment and shrugged. "Don't take it seriously. It's just a silly test they give to grad students."

"Yeah, right. I can always go back through that wall of yours and start the test all over again, huh?"

She nodded, but when I closed my eyes again, the opening in the wall was gone. It was six thirty in the morning and I was hung-over, getting ready to go to the Adjustment Center.

I never saw that woman again but once in a while, doing the count in the yard, I would look down the line of inmates and for a second see myself at the end.

Her little test was weird. I don't know what it meant, or if it meant anything at all. San Quentin does weird things to the mind.

-#-

9

Gangrene

After a few years at San Quentin, I could read the dictionary of inmates pretty well. But the more I read, the more alarmed I got. There were just so many of them, and so few of us correctional officers. I started seeing myself as a candle trying to make a difference inside a cave so big it always seemed to grow bigger and darker every time I looked inside. "What good am I doing here?" I began asking myself on the tier, or inside the Adjustment Center, or escorting an inmate through Death Row. I knew that no correctional officer would ever start working at a prison if he had such a question in his mind.

I had to train myself to stop thinking such thoughts, because I knew the inmates would come to see the doubt in my eyes. I had to constantly tell myself I was making a difference. I kept bad people from getting out and doing harm. It didn't stack up to much when compared to a doctor or an engineer, but it was all I had to help me believe that I was doing good, no matter how little good it was.

At a body builder competition, all the contestants look strong. The differences are subtle, but one person will always stand out. It is the same with inmates. One will always stand out as champion gladiator, the born leader. At San Quentin, his name was George Winters, or G. W., as he preferred. His wish was everyone's command, even the correctional officers'. No one wanted to mess with G. W. He had arms as big as fire hoses, and power enough to reach into the hood and have you or any member of your family taken out. Guilty of multiple murders and a resident of Death Row, G. W. had managed to achieve international renown by pleading for warring gangs to make peace. He told reporters he wanted to stop the senseless shootings claiming the lives of too many young African-Americans.

In interviews made over the phone from Death Row, G. W. had said that violence was no longer in his vocabulary. Many people, including correctional officers, thought that he must have gone through a spiritual transformation—having been so close to execution time after time. But G. W.'s change of heart was either short-lived or a ruse to get his death sentence commuted to life. He had been losing one appeal after another and was becoming more aware that his execution was going to be carried out. One of his "kites" had been interrupted. A forbidden form of communication in prison those notes are attached to string and tossed down the tiers. There are little knots in the string showing who the "kite" is intended for. If there are three knots in one part of the string, it means Tier 3, and another five in another part indicates Cell 5.

Whoever sends the kite has to try to get it near the right cell. In practice, an inmate seeing a "kite" land outside his cell is supposed to pass it on. But the sender never knows who might find it. A note from a Mexican calling for a stabbing against a white might be intercepted by an Aryan Nation member. It is a risky way to pass secrets—but it is the only one the inmates have in lock-up.

Inmates would only throw "kites" when correctional officers left the tiers, and then they would make the air look like a giant white spider web: There would be fifty or sixty spooling through the air. We used to sneak back in and watch them, and then, like cats leaping at string, we'd rush out, trying to grab as many "kites" as we could.

"Cop on the tier!," a voice would shout from a cell.

In an instant inmates would be yanking them in. Within moments, all the "kites" would have vanished ... except for the few we'd snagged. In G. W.'s case, one of his kites was intercepted by a correctional officer before it could be passed along to the gang member it was intended for.

In his note, G. W. said that if he was executed all bets were off. His "homies" were ordered to go after certain staff members and inmates. Mine was one of the names on the list. The warden had G. W. quickly moved up north, to a prison that functioned like a holding area for San Quentin prisoners who had been moved for one reason or another.

Once his execution date approached, G. W. would be returned to Death Row. Until then, he would sit in isolation up north ... where he could do the least harm.

I had first met G. W. on Death Row. When I started at San Quentin, I was told by older officers that there would be incidents when I would have to "stand up" or I would be walked over during my entire career. If I backed down from an inmate, my cowardice wouldn't be confined to me. It could tarnish the reputation of the other officers, too. An officer who "peed all over himself" was a risk for all the other staff. The inmates would know that an officer had backed down, and from then on they would be all over him and every one else that officer was close to.... which is why it was fatal for an officer to give in to fear. He would be an exile—marooned between the other officers and the inmates. Fair game, in other words.

I had never "pissed on myself" from fear, even during my worst moments with my father. I wasn't going to start behind the walls.

A couple weeks later I was escorting G. W. to the showers at Death Row. Because of his size and strength, he was handcuffed and had his legs shackled. Along the way, he stopped to say something to one of the other condemned men. Inmates aren't allowed to stop. It is a major infraction of the rules. I was on over-time and edgy from lack of sleep. He may have decided to test the new officer, and I could have chosen a better way to respond. "Hey, man, you know what the rules are. Get your ass moving."

"What'd you say?"

"You heard me, move."

"You know who the fuck you're talking to?"

"Yeah, I'm talking to an inmate at San Quentin. Now get moving back to your house."

"Hey, motherfucker, I could kill you right now for disrespect."

"Yeah, whatever," I said, moving forward to grab him.

With one flex of arms thick as strips of tires, he snapped both handcuffs.

As huge as he was, G. W. grew even bigger in front of me, like a bellows filling out.

I moved to grab him, but he yanked one leg back, breaking the shackle. Now he has both arms and his legs free. But I wasn't going to let him run me off Death Row. As I started toward him, he grabbed me and threw me down the tier. I banged against a cell and slid to the floor. I could see the gunman heading down the railing, his pistol in his hand.

"Hold off," I yelled, getting back on my feet.

I went forward, and again G. W. tossed me aside like an empty cardboard box.

Whistles were blowing, and more officers were running down the tier. I could tell the gunman was ready to fire at any moment. I motioned for all of them to stand back.

Twice more G. W. tossed me back down the tier. Then, with a big grin, he dropped his hands to his side. "Good work," he said, turning to allow himself to be handcuffed.

Minutes later, he was back in his cuffs and shackles, and I continued escorting him to his cell. "Hey, man," he called out, "were you scared when I had you back there?"

"Honestly, no. I had it coming. You're right, I did disrespect you. I should never have talked to you like that in front of one of your 'homies.'"

G. W. nodded. "Yeah."

"But no matter what I did, G. W., you weren't gonna run me off my tier. This may be where you live, but this is my home, too."

We never had another problem.

An old sergeant told me that in prison respect is like a razor blade that two men use to shave each other. Trust is a big part of it … but you can't be squeamish when that blade touches your throat, or it'll be cut.

Once I got G. W. into his cell, I went down to the officers' bathroom and pissed out what I refused to piss in my pants. I had been scared, not so much of G. W., but of my father. When G. W. threw me back, I saw myself falling backward in our kitchen when my father was in one of his rages. I washed my face and looked in the mirror. Maybe I had stood up not only for the correctional officer I was, but for the boy I had been.

As though to remind me of my past, my father came back into my life a few weeks later; like so many times before, he appeared because of mistaken identity: his, mine, ours.

I was standing watch inside the Armory Tower at San Quentin, a post locked from the inside and from the outside, and with a ramp that is raised whenever a guard goes inside to stand watch. The tower is then isolated like a castle in the middle of a moat. No one can get in or out without a key first being lowered from the turret to bring down the ramp to let the relief guard open the gate leading up to the stairs to the top.

I was working a double-shift when the phone rang. It was the captain's office.

"Hey, who's up there?" asked a lieutenant.

I thought he was being a smart ass. "Who the hell do you think's up here? The same guy who was up here when he checked in at four in the evening."

"Is this Woolf?"

"No, it's Mickey Mouse. Now I gotta go. I'm busy." I think I added that I was using the toilet, when I was really in the midst of hearing a really good song on my portable radio. Radios weren't allowed in any of the guard towers, but we would bring them in anyway to help us stay awake, especially when working sixteen hours: two back-to-back, eight-hour shifts.

"Okay. We just wanted to make sure you were up there, because we just heard over the San Rafael Police Department scanner that a Rudy Woolf has stolen a cab."

"Well, it's not me."

A little while later, the phone rang again. "Are you still there?"

"Hey, you just checked in with me half an hour ago. What the hell is the problem?"

"We just gotta be certain you're up there," said the Lieutenant. "We just got a phone call. I gotta ask you a question. You're Rudy. J. Woolf, right? J. as in John?"

"Yeah, I'm Rudy J. Woolf. Why?"

There was a pause. "Then there are two of you. You know another person with the same name?"

"Yeah, my dad. It can't be my grandfather since he's dead. He had the same name, too. What's up?"

"We just got a phone call that your dad apparently took some driver's cab and disappeared with it."

I had no idea what the hell the lieutenant was talking about. "I don't know where my father might have gone. And to be honest, I don't care."

When I got off work, I went to my father's house to find out what had happened. Because of numerous drunk driving violations, my father had lost his driver's license. If my father wanted to do something, he'd do it. No matter what. Nothing would stop him. He had wanted to have some fun so he called for a cab and had the driver take him to the Barrel House, a bar in San Rafael. My father invited the driver in for a drink, then a second one. About two hours later, they went to another bar where they picked up two women. My father convinced the cab driver to take the two women back to his place. Once they got there, the cab driver started making moves on the woman he was with. My father told him, "Why don't you take her in my bedroom and fuck her? When you're done, I'll be scoring with mine. Then you can take 'em back and dump them."

The cab driver took the woman with him back to the bedroom and started screwing. But my father didn't do so well. The woman he was with didn't want to put out. So he told her to take a hike. Angry, the woman called out for her friend to come with her, but the other woman didn't want to leave. So my father said he'd take the woman he was with back to town in the taxi. While he was out, he decided to go by a liquor store and then stop for a little breakfast. On his way to the restaurant, somebody saw the cab and hailed him down. My father took the guy where he wanted to go, collected the fare, and even got a tip. Soon, he was driving all over Marin County, picking up fares and collecting money. Around this time, the cab driver woke up and found his cab gone. Panicking, he called the San Rafael Police Department.

About seven in the morning, the police spotted the stolen taxi and started chasing it, but my father wouldn't pull over. He just slowed down to about thirty, not to exceed the speed limit. He sure as hell didn't want to get a ticket for speeding. He drove back to his house and parked the cab. As he got out, four cops jumped him, for the word was out about my father. He had developed a reputation: If you're gonna arrest Rudy Woolf, you had better send several cops. He was wrestled to the ground, handcuffed, and taken to jail. The police left the cab for the driver, who had to take another taxi to get his own back. But he hadn't sobered up enough, and within minutes of leaving my father's house the driver got into an accident and was arrested for drunken driving.

Once again, on the front page of the <u>Marin Independent Journal</u> appeared the name Rudy Woolf.

A few days later my father appeared in court. The cab driver and the attorney for the taxi company did everything they could to have my father found guilty of auto theft. But my father started telling his side of the story, complete with the women they met and took back to his house. Within moments the judge was laughing, and promptly threw out the charge.

It wasn't just the story that got my father off. It was from his being connected. He had friends in the judicial branch within Marin County and the state of California. Some of the judges used to go out and drink and raise hell with my father. It's what being connected means.

My father skated out over ice that anybody else would have fallen through and drowned under. I wondered if maybe his reason for naming me after him and his own father had more to do with carrying on a curse than continuing the family name. Of course, in my case they were the same thing.

-#-

10

Inventory

Searching a cell, I always started in the back and worked my way to the front, checking everything—beginning with the inside of the toilet bowl, and then checking the porcelain on the outside for scratch marks that indicate a weapon was being sharpened on it. I inspected the heater vent to see that it wasn't being worked loose. I always made certain each bar was unmarked by a hacksaw or wire working its way, slowly, over weeks and months, through steel. I made sure the screen over the bars was tight to prevent spears from being thrust. Like an obsessive person looking for something he can't find but knows is there, I would work my way from one cell to the next—shaking open books, sorting through legal documents and letters filling cardboard boxes, feeling inside shoes and pulling on heels, looking for any sign that something was amiss. I even reached inside sleeves and turned socks inside out. Hours were spent working my way down one tier. The spoils of my hunt: inmate-made knives, spears, picks, screwdrivers, sharpened ends of mop handles, iron rods, razor blades, shards of plastic mirror, razor blades. I turned up knives and pistols fashioned from Bic pens with ground-up match heads for powder, a rubber band for a spring, a paper clip for a detonator, and a ball of hardened cereal dipped in excrement for a bullet.

To remind me that I was never out of range, a blow gun would turn up from time to time. Finders, keepers, I always said.

-#-

11

Ghost Marriage

Always slender, Amy had grown thinner and was now gaunt. It made no sense to me why my wife was starving herself. I had always made sure there was plenty of food, even during the hard days at the beginning of our marriage when I had to steal groceries from Safeway. Day by day, she was fading away. Doctors didn't know what was wrong with her. Medication and therapy weren't curing her. They were merely keeping her in a holding pattern from disappearing completely. Nights I'd come in from working overtime and find her hollow silhouette lying in bed, with her shoulder blades and rib cage protruding from under her skin. One morning I opened the bathroom cabinet and counted seventeen vials of medicine. I knew above all I had to keep my medical coverage. It seemed to be the only thing that would keep her alive. It never occurred to me that she had gone inside the frail walls of her body just as I had gone behind the stone walls of San Quentin … except that I, unlike Amy, would come back before leaving again. She just kept on going. It would have done no good for her to turn to my family or hers for help. Amy and I were like members of warring medieval clans—cut off from all contact with our individual families unless we broke with each other and returned to our folds. To compound Amy's isolation, I kept accepting overtime, leaving her for longer and longer stretches alone with the baby. It was a sad, stupid pattern we had developed, like one of those Swiss clocks where one figure would be coming out as the other was going in.

We were marooned together—with nobody calling for help.

If our weight could be a measurement of how we felt, then we were hurling in opposite directions: Amy, who at her peak weighed 110, dropped to 75 pounds at her lowest. Me, I was out to win the Pillsbury Dough Boy Award—shooting from my regular weight of 200 up to 310. And the more I told her to eat, the less she would; conversely, the more she told me to start going on a diet, the more I ate. It was a recipe for disaster. One of the worst things about getting locked into a pattern is that real time gets lost and some weird repetitious pattern takes its place.

I couldn't believe I had put in three years at San Quentin. Amy and I were like statues wheeled in front of each other for a few hours every night. They didn't speak. They didn't make love. And in the morning, the statues would be separated again. I knew things were bad, but I didn't want to talk about it. Neither did Amy. She had her woman's group now, which I called the Banshees, to hear her complaints and share stories with about the jerks they were married to.

When I was home, I took care of groceries, the rent, and paying the bills, but I wasn't there in the way a husband and father should have been. Amy finally reached the lowest weight possible without being hospitalized. For months she remained the same: emaciated, pale, listless. The food I bought for her wasn't being touched. I didn't know when she did eat—at least with her women friends. Amy was still driving around in the jalopy we had when we first got married, so I bought her a new car, thinking it might cheer her up. A flicker of interest—then back to the same apathy.

Medical specialists kept telling her that there was nothing physically wrong with her. Since she had never lost so much weight before, she figured the stress had to be coming from her marriage; and since it couldn't be Gail causing the problem, she figured it had to be me. A crazy logic, but it made sense to her. She went from one prescription to another—trying to find the one that would cure her of me, or whatever was wrong with us.

It didn't help that Amy's mother kept telling her wives shouldn't be slaves to their husbands. Every time she learned that Amy had made dinner or done something to try to brighten the apartment, she came down on her for being a modern slave: a housewife. Not mincing words, her mother called Amy a loser for staying with me because of Gail. It created a tremendous pull on Amy, who had wanted children. She knew her mother wasn't to be trusted—but her female friends, in a more sensitive, articulate manner, were saying the same thing as her mother: Leave him.

And if Amy needed to verify what the women said about me was true, all she had to do was come home and see how I was behaving—if I was there. As for getting to know the wives of other correctional officers, Amy refused. She wanted nothing to do with the prison or anyone, beside me, who had anything to do with it. A protracted sadness took over. My other family seemed to vanish about this time, too.

For some reason I was never able to fathom, my father got hired as a salesman for a major radio station in Santa Barbara. Basically, he had to get out of Marin County because things were so hot for him—so he called in a marker.

Like the Pied Piper, he called almost all the others to follow him, and he led them south: Griff, Kelly, Doris, and Mandy. Gina was in a marriage hell of her own and thinking about divorcing her husband for having an affair. She had to remain behind in Marin County. Once Kelly and Doris started planning the trip to Santa Barbara, they told me to leave Amy, take Gail, and join them. "No way," I thought. I wasn't going to walk away from my marriage like it was a restaurant where I didn't like the food. Amy and I had a child. We couldn't let Gail grow up as we had, each with a missing parent, and end up as we had. We had to stick it out. Yet the life we led together told otherwise. Whenever I came home and found the babysitter, I knew that Amy was off with the Banshees, so I would go drink at Zimm's or The Barrel Room. There was always a woman at the bar willing to listen to my woes. I didn't like going home to an empty house, even if I was the one supplying the emptiness.

Therapists in those days were for people with major problems. I sure wasn't going to admit I had any. If I had sought help at San Quentin, I would have been considered a security risk and pulled from the overtime shifts. That would have thrown us into a worse situation than the one we were already in. With Amy not working, we needed every dollar I could make.

What's the world's record for a couple going nowhere without admitting they have reached a dead end? I don't know, but we might have set it. Someone had to blink to save the marriage. And someone did, but it wasn't Amy and it wasn't me.

We had another child, a son. I made certain he would not be named after three previous generations of Rudy Woolf. He would be called Brian.

My father and Amy's mother said we were crazy to have another child. Things would only get worse. But seeing Amy holding the baby, with Gail smiling at her little brother, hit me. It was like an untaken photograph of the family I wanted to have; then I realized I had them, but unless something was done quickly, I was going to lose them.

Amy must have decided to give me another chance, for her disposition changed. Amy was very strong. She had to be to have survived the malignant selfishness of her mother. But like a prize fighter who gets stunned in the ring, Amy had somehow gotten turned around, punching thin air first, and then herself. Now, she was back in front of me—letting me know she cared. For the first time in months she was warm and responsive.

I tried to show her I saw the change, but I discovered that I had lost the way of recognizing and responding to love. I couldn't blame it on working at San Quentin—but working there hadn't helped. All the ways I had of responding to affection were damaged; thus I was damaging Amy in turn. I knew the only way for me to grow was to quit thinking the way my father had taught me to think: seeing every exchange in terms of what I could get for myself. I had to pluck my father's psyche out of my own, but like drawing salt from sea water, it was an arduous task. But no matter how much I wanted to be open with Amy, I knew that I couldn't be with the inmates ... or the officers.

I couldn't turn up at San Quentin telling the other officers, let alone the inmates, that I wanted to be open and honest from then on. If I hadn't been fired on the spot, I would have been seen as weak by the inmates, and devoured. No, I had to keep tough in one world and be open in the other. It was a horrible split. Something was always getting lost in the transition from my job to my home. I kept telling myself that being a correctional officer was just about wearing a mask. But masks don't come off that easily, and mine was stuck to my face.

I needed friends then, but not ones with drinks in hand. I wanted a brother I could talk to, not one who was either racing on speed or so stoned on downers that his words slurred and he drooled. It was a form of emotional subtraction: separating myself from the guards, then from my family, until only one person was left ... the one who was there all along: I asked Amy to help me.

It was as though she had been waiting for me to ask, for she came forward and brought every bit of her intelligence and judgment to light on me.

I quit drinking, quit hanging out with the guys from prison, and started pulling back on the overtime, but something was happening—as though every time I would come in sober and find the house clean, dinner on the table, and Gail helping feed Brian in the highchair, I would panic. It was too much of a family for someone who had grown up with so little of one. I fled like a creature into the night. The light hurt.

Amy didn't need another or a group of friends to say, "See, what did we tell you?" She could see for herself that I was gone again. And she took her little Make-Me-Invisible pill again.

That's when the fist fights started. I'd be drinking with officers from work when someone down the bar would make a crack, and the next thing I knew they'd be pulling me off the hapless guy. Prison toxins were seeping into me. The little bit of power I had as a correctional officer was a muscle I kept flexing to make me stronger and stronger. I think if I had met myself back then, I would have thought, "What an asshole." After a few drinks, I started becoming another Rudy J. Woolf, one my father would have been proud of.

Countless times I would swear to leave San Quentin behind me at the gate and not think about what I had seen on the tier—but even if I could take a shower to wash off the grime, I couldn't shower the inside of my head.

All day I would be seeing pornographic photographs in the cells. Inmates had them everywhere: men with women, women with women, men with men, and ones with kids (those torn up and scattered on the floor every time I turned them up).

Once searching a man's pillow, I stuck my hand inside a hole to make sure there wasn't any contraband, and suddenly my hand was sticky with cum from where the inmate had been using the pillow as a vagina.

Moments like those started hardening me to whatever I did or saw. I did everything I could to keep San Quentin from affecting me, but it was like being in a fire and saying the flames weren't going to burn me. Bullshit. I was on fire. And the only way I could save myself was by sealing myself off in my own asbestos suit. I saw what could happen if I didn't have one on. We caught officers masturbating to photographs in some of the magazines they had seized. Pretty sad, I thought—gotta "fuck" an inmate's girlfriend. And in contrast to the element of fire, the little water torture of San Quentin, day after day, week after week, was doing its job. I was getting a little too comfortable overseeing the lives of so many men. I could tell that the little taste of power—being able to search a man anytime I wanted, being able to toss his cell on the slightest suspicion—was making me giddy. Hell, if someone had given me enough grief, I could have planted dope in his cell to double the time he had left. I didn't—but knowing I could was like a weapon I wouldn't use unless I had to.

I worked out an unspoken truce with the inmates. I let them know I would be fair if they followed the rules. Being white made no difference in how I treated whites, blacks, or Hispanics or Indians for that matter. They were all the same to me—if they did their time. But if they fucked with me, they knew I would make their lives a thousand times more miserable when I was done. A poor job-attitude—but it went with the territory.

Everybody but Amy knew me as outgoing, brash, fun-loving at best, wild at worst. "A classic extrovert" was how a teacher described me to her girlfriend after meeting me when I was out for some fun. But I felt surprised, as though she was talking about someone else. That's not me, I thought, I'm an introvert—but there wasn't much evidence of it in my life. And when I looked at the seven thousand involuntary residents of San Quentin, I thought, "This is what I am."

Gina finally broke up with her own husband. She was too hurt to tell me. My father called up in a jovial mood, saying that Gina had gotten rid of "the asshole." I knew what he was happy about: Just as Amy had taken me away from my family, so Gina's husband had taken her away—and now Gina would be coming back to the family. What my father and my siblings didn't realize and would never have accepted is that I took myself away from them. The handwriting on the wall was one word: WOOLF.

Now that Gina had gone back to living with my father, he started putting more pressure on me to leave "the bitch," as he referred to Amy. She, in turn, hated my father, but she desperately had wanted to make friends with my sisters and brother. Loyalty reared its stiff head. Kelly and the others couldn't be friends with Amy without incurring the wrath of my father, so they rejected each overture she made toward them. If Amy felt contempt for my father because of what he had done while I was in the Army, what he did next pushed her away forever.

Knowing that Amy had been using a public laundry to wash our clothes, her grandmother bought her a washer and dryer. These gifts arrived just as we were getting ready to move into another apartment. We didn't have space for the appliances until we moved into our new home, so I asked Kelly if I could leave them at her house. She was happy to help us, she said.

A few days after the move, I went to get the machines. They were gone. My father, I learned, had taken them off and sold them—giving Kelly part of the money. I couldn't help laughing. It was like the worst practical joke I had ever heard of being played on someone, but it wasn't a joke, and the victim was Amy. When Amy heard me laugh, she looked like she had fainted inside herself. I did everything to get the washer and dryer back—but as with many things my father had done, it was too late.

I told a buddy at work what my father had done, "He's a real prick," he responded.

"Yeah, but he's a lovable prick," I said, hating myself the instant I heard what I had said.

I couldn't get away from the horrible mixture of love and hate I felt for him. I despised what he did to Amy and me, but somewhere inside me was a weird feeling of approval. I could never have told Amy about my divided emotions for my father.

The next time I saw my father I told him he had better not ever do anything like that again.

He laughed his strange, guilty-little-boy-proud-of-being-caught laugh, the laugh that I know I inherited. I wanted to tear that laugh from inside me. I just didn't know what to do—except to not laugh.

Amy told me that nothing fazed my father. She was right. He was like onyx; everything bounced off him. I had never known him to apologize. I had never known him to say he was sorry. I had never known him to question himself and who he was.

One night I had a dream of a village being destroyed from explosions; all of the people in the village were fleeing, and in the midst of all destruction here comes my father, strolling through the debris as though out for a walk. Then I realized he was the blast … he was causing all the destruction. I'm glad I woke up.

A few weeks later, I got drunk and gave him a piece of my mind. He flung it back. For ten minutes he hurled every obscenity at me.

When he finished, I smiled. "Hey, you think you can insult me? I've been insulted by the worst. I've had things said to me that would make a whore's ears bleed."

"Yeah, yeah," was all he could say.

Poor Griff. I was too preoccupied with my own problems with my father to see the ones my brother was having with him. When my mother was alive, she acted as a buffer between my father and the children. Her death removed the only protection we had. Being the oldest, I moved up and tried to take her place—as best I could. But then I left for the Army, and Griff found himself faced off with my father. He wasn't strong enough to fight back. I don't know if it came from feeling responsible for our mother's death by telling her he wanted her to die, but Griff was trapped in a no-man's land between wanting my father's respect and giving up a life of his own, or going off to find a life of his own, as I had done, and risking our father's wrath. He tried to have it both ways, which meant he fell between the two.

'What do you think of Griff?" I asked Gina.

"Road kill," she uttered, too quickly for me to believe Gina really meant what she said. Even so, I was shocked by the harshness of her words.

When I told Amy what Gina had said about my brother, she nodded. "What do you expect?"

"What does that mean?" I shouted, loud enough for a neighbor to bang on the wall.

"Nothing," she whispered and went into the bedroom, closing the door.

Feeling the apartment squeezing around me, I drove over to San Francisco. Dropping the car off at a parking lot, I wandered into a strip club called Pandora's Box in Union Square. When they weren't performing, the dancers were out mingling with the customers, getting them to buy more drinks, and getting a commission for themselves at the end of the night. A gorgeous redhead sat down and started talking to me. I bought her champagne and ordered a straight vodka for myself. We talked, laughed, and went on drinking and laughing and talking.

Everything jagged smoothed out. It was like she had been sent to take my mind off everything: Amy, my father, Griff, most of all San Quentin. As with Amy the night we met, Diane and I talked until dawn; then I got her phone number and drove back for duty inside my circle of Hell.

-#-

12

Punch Lines

It wasn't all grimness and darkness. There was laughter, too, working at San Quentin. Three incidents stand out. The first dealt with an inmate with an unusual nickname. Shitty Long was his name, and it was no figure of speech. A violent inmate, he had spent months in the Secure Housing Unit where, when in a bad mood, he would coat himself with excrement and refuse to come out of his cell for shower call. All the officers dreaded the order to extract Shitty, for he would be waiting to hurl fresh turds at them. No matter how hard they tried to use their inverted U-shaped shields to cuff Shitty's entire body to keep him from getting near, he always managed to slip through and soil the officers. Yet there were times when Shitty didn't live up to his name, and, without joking, I wanted to get on his good side. I went out of my way to treat him with respect, never once lecturing him on his lack of personal hygiene. An extra apple or portion of pudding didn't hurt either. It wasn't long before we had worked out a code. If Shitty was in a bad mood, he'd let me know.

"Hey, Mr. Long, it's me," I'd call out, before rolling the food cart within range of his cell.

"Come on down, Woolf."

"Sure you're okay?"

"No shit," he'd say, and mean it ... I hoped.

The second funny incident involved my only flirtatious encounter with a female behind bars. She was the secretary I met in the captain's office in Vacaville, where I had gone to turn in some paper work after escorting an inmate from San Quentin. She was really cute and started asking me all about myself. I guess I was flattered to have such an attractive woman coming on to me, for when she asked me for my phone number, I gave it to her—well, my cell phone number anyway. I didn't want a woman calling me at home. As I was finished I decided, what the hell, why not stay around Vacaville and have a drink with her. I asked the secretary what time she was getting off.

"Sorry, hon, I'd love to, but I'm booked tonight," she said.

After telling her to give me a call some time, I left. When I was almost to the Vallejo-San Rafael Bridge, my cell phone rang. I thought it might be the secretary. Instead, it was the captain from Vacaville. He wanted to inform me that the secretary to whom I had given my phone number was first, an inmate, and second, wasn't a she at all—but a transsexual who had undergone a gender transformation while at Vacaville. And Roberta, once Robert, was doing twenty years for an armed robbery committed while a man. I almost swerved off the road. That wasn't the end of it. When I got back to San Quentin, I was told to report to the captain on watch. When I got to his office, he asked me how the transportation detail had gone.

"Fine," I answered.

"Hear you met some chick at Vacaville."

I played dumb, which sometimes isn't hard to do.

"Did you notice what she was wearing?" he asked.

"Huh?"

"Did you notice that blue denim shirt she had on?"

"She wasn't wearing a blue shirt."

"You want me to call Vacaville and ask the captain?"

Damn, he knew. "Well, I wasn't paying too much attention. She might have had on a flimsy blue thing ... kinda off the shoulder."

Just then the loud speaker squawked. "Will Lover Boy Woolf please report to the Warden's Office? An inmate at Vacaville with a really high voice wants to talk to you." For a second, I was terrified that the warden had been told what I had done. But a moment later, the lieutenant started laughing and said to stop giving out my phone number to inmates, whatever the gender. He said I was lucky my romantic encounter got "nipped in the bud."

I was lucky I had escaped with a warning. What if the secretary had been released that day, had called me, and I had met her for the drink? I shuddered and put the he-she out of my mind.

During my time at San Quentin, I got to know other transsexuals, all of whom were kept separate from the male prison population, for obvious reasons, before being transferred up to Vacaville, where there was a special unit for them. Some transsexuals were midway in the transition from one sex to the other: with budding breasts yet still with male genitals. They had been sentenced to prison before being able to complete the sexual transformation. In California, they were lucky, for the operation would be performed at no cost to the inmate.

One Valentine's Day, three such inmates were awaiting transportation. I felt sorry for them, stuck off in an isolation unit. They had been getting all made up in their cells, putting on shirts that they had knotted at the tails and made to look like halters, and rolled up at the waist to look more feminine. The longest time was spent with the makeup. They did wonders to their cheeks and eyebrows with crayons. But for all their efforts to look glamorous on Valentine's Day, they had nowhere to go to show off and be appreciated.

When I got my lunch break, I drove into Larkspur and bought three carnations. I would have preferred roses, but they're not allowed in prison; when soaked in urine, they harden and can be used as spears. I took the three red carnations back and went up on the block to deliver them. The trio was ecstatic. They gushed and preened around their cells, holding up the flowers as though getting bouquets from their boyfriends.

"Oh, thank you, Sweet Rudy," one exclaimed.

I laughed, not just at the pleasure I had brought them, but at thinking what my father would say if he heard his namesake called Sweet Rudy.

"Nothing sweet about him," he would have snorted. "Like father, like son.'

He was wrong. I wasn't him. I was myself—but who that was, I still wasn't sure.

-#-

13

Prison Lore

Ever since I started at San Quentin, people outside the walls kept asking me why I became a prison guard. I really didn't know myself well enough to answer; besides, I don't think they were really interested in hearing what I would have said. Their questions were more of a judgment—like, why of all professions become a prison guard? The difference between the two questions was, for me anyway, between understanding and contempt. Underneath it all … it is a fair question, for who the hell wants to go to work behind walls and guard people who have done the worst imaginable things to other human beings and will do the same to you if given the chance? Guards, the reasoning goes, must be into some sadistic power trip or be brain-dead—sometimes both at the same time. It wasn't by accident that a guard used to be called "Bull."

I've seen a lot of prison movies, from the ones in the 30's like <u>Scarface</u>, <u>My Six Convicts</u>, and <u>White Lightning</u>, and those more recent, like <u>Shawshank Redemption</u> and <u>The Green Mile.</u> All portray guards as knuckle-dragging behemoths who move like the Jolly Green Giant—thud, thud, thud—on their way from beating one prisoner to the next.

Slowly, the archetype of the guard has altered. He is no longer a stern-faced mute with a potato face and pot belly, swinging a Rudy-club, like the lead-filled ones used at San Quentin until the 1950's. Even today, the correctional officer is portrayed as a spiritless non-entity who, like a career soldier during a time of peace, just wants to draw a salary and count off the days until retirement and pension.

Who in his right mind would want to work inside a maximum security prison and risk being stabbed by spears, smeared with feces or shot by guns made from Bic pens and paperclips? Who but someone who can't do anything else in life? I guess it was true of me for a long time. It wasn't that I couldn't hold down other jobs. I had been … life insurance salesman, tow truck driver, store clerk, even security guard. But I lacked the one quality that would have allowed me to have a career: self-confidence. Ironically, that same quality I lacked was the essential one for survival in prison. Every day when I went up on the tiers I felt like I was trying to fool the inmates into believing I was someone I was not. Maybe the mask I wore was good enough to fool them, or maybe the mask became the face behind it. I don't know. But the last place in the world I should have gone to find self-esteem was also the worst: first, because by not having it I made myself a target; second, because nobody was handing out self-esteem at San Quentin. All the inmates were holding on to the little they had—like virgins in a harem.

Slowly, though, with each confrontation avoided with words, with each weapon taken away peacefully, I knew that I was changing. San Quentin was my real education, my own private college, with thousands of unforgiving teachers. If I had told old-timer guards how I saw San Quentin, they would have laughed and avoided me from then on. I would have been seen as embodying the new school of officers, with their warped aspirations of bringing ideas of rehabilitation behind the walls. For guards of the old school, San Quentin was an enormous warehouse where you stored things that didn't belong anywhere else, and you did whatever it took, including beating and killing, to make sure they stayed there.

Yet I was a hybrid, a member of the first graduating class from the California Correctional Officers Academy. Rather than learn the ropes from the old-timers at San Quentin, I had to learn them on my own ... for the old-school guards wanted to show us they knew what we could never learn in a classroom but only on the tiers. It was difficult at times to know which way was right—the old or the new, for sometimes they were contradictory—and you had to choose which way you were going to react. And all the time you were choosing, you knew the old guards and the new were watching to see, like with the gangs, where you were going to line up. You could be sure, if the guards were watching, from some hidden vantage point the inmates were, too. Something that used to drive me crazy was thinking that no matter where I went inside the walls, I always felt out of view of the prisoners as long as I was in view of the guards, but once I moved out of their line of sight, every prisoner seemed to see me vulnerable and alone.

One of the major changes that occurred when the old gave way to the new was the diminishing contact with inmates. Back in the era of prisoners and guards, officers got to know each inmate. The guard didn't have to go running up to his superiors to find out how to take care of a problem. He could handle it himself, not always the right way or the kind way, but his way.

That method had changed. Now every incident had to be written down, and in triplicate. Officers spent more time filling out forms for an incident than walking the tiers. Paperwork weighed down every shift. Outside the walls, society had changed, and those changes were appearing in the prison.

The American Civil Liberties Union (ACLU) brought about major changes by going to the Supreme Court to argue for the rights of prisoners. Laws on racial equality that were enacted in society at large became integrated into prison existence. And that wasn't all that changed. Public perception changed. Prisoners were now perceived as victims of society. Psychologists talked about the role of childhood in contributing to the character of a criminal. Guards weren't helping their case, for every time a brutality or corruption scandal would occur, people would shake their heads. "They're worse than the people they guard," they'd say. And politicians would pass new laws strengthening the rights of the prisoners but diluting those of the guards.

Not only did the officers have to learn their new responsibilities, but the prisoners also had to learn how far they could go with their new rights. A line was crossed. It would be like imagining the yellow line in the yard, the dead line, started to move closer and closer to the guards patrolling along the wall, then up against the wall itself, so that the guards no longer had a space an inmate would only cross at risk of death.

Before, convicts never came within arm's reach of a guard. If they did, they could be struck with a blow from his truncheon. Arm's length was the distance a knife could reach. Back then, guards moved inside their own invisible yellow line that inmates knew not to cross—and they what would happen when they did. Now the line was gone, and violence against officers was soaring. To worsen matters, the old-time felons with their code of justice, harsh but fair, were being replaced by young "gang bangers," whose amoral code was ruled by impulse.

Doing shifts in the Reception Center, I would watch busloads of new inmates arrive. Called "Fish' because they had been caught, these new prisoners were truculent, coiled, and menacing. There was no deference in their eyes toward the old-timers. In fact, they didn't conceal the contempt they had for everyone except their "homies."

Soon the rule of the old-time prisoners, too, was overturned. The balance between the old-timers and the young gang members was gone; not long afterward, the gang members were running things. The old inmates, some of whom had come in thirty or forty years before on life without parole, found themselves fearing for their lives over nothing they had done ... but simply because of who they were.

A figure shoots through me like an ice pick: ninety percent of today's maximum prison population is gang-affiliated. The only old-timers left alive at San

Quentin are either working in the hospital or staying to themselves. Prison gangs rule prison.

After working about eighteen months inside the prison, I became a member of the Emergency Rescue Team, a SWAT unit inside the prison. If the institution were ever taken over, we'd come in by helicopter, rappel down by rope, blow the roof, and go into the block with orders to kill anything that moved. If it was a guard, it was a guard; and if it was an inmate, it was an inmate. Since the takeover of the Adjustment Center by George Jackson and two accomplices in 1971, no quarter had been given on either side.

The warden would do all he could to get you out—but no prisoner was going to successfully walk past the walls using you as a shield for freedom. You knew the policy going in. You were on your own. The only firearms were on up the gun rails and in the towers. Inside the prison, the only protection a correctional officer had was his brass whistle. If he blew it, all available guards would come running to help him—if he was still alive.

Amy used to ask me, "What should I do if you're ever taken hostage?"

She finally got tired of my shrugging. "I mean it. What do I do?"

"Dig out my life-insurance policy, and make sure my tie doesn't clash with the lining of my casket."

"Oh, stop it. I'm serious," she said.

I couldn't help smiling. "So am I."

She quit asking.

-#-

14

Those Who Also Wait

The inmate's name was Small and he was anything but. Another officer and I were working in the Adjustment Center and it was time for Small to get his shower. Small was naked in his cell, having been handed out the toilet articles and towel he was allowed to take to the shower. We told him the procedure: Hold up your hands, lift the folds of your belly, and run your hands through your hair, which in Small's case wasn't necessary since he was bald. Then he was told to turn around, bend over, and cough so we could check that his rectum was clean, at least when it came to concealing a weapon.

Then he "cuffed up," meaning he backed up to the cell door, extending his hands through the food slot, so that we could put handcuffs on him, rendering him less of a threat.

Small was cooperative, which was good, because if there was ever a model for the joke about the 500 pound gorilla, it was Small. As I knew well, names are weird, always providing life-long jokes on the people who have them. I had black inmates named White and white inmates named Black. There was a Jesus who was a Hell's Angel, and a Meek who was anything but. As I told myself, what's in a name? Everything and nothing. In Small's case, not much. The last time he had been small was probably in the crib.

After we arrived at the foot port just outside the shower area, which is itself enclosed within a cell, we let him enter the shower area, and we uncuffed him. Everything went fine for about twenty minutes; then Small told Officer Chase he wanted to get out. So Chase told him to "cuff up."

Then it happened. In the moment that Small stepped backwards to the food port opening to be cuffed up and Chase opened the cell and leaned forward to put him in handcuffs, Small managed to pull a home-made knife out of his rectum and stab Chase in the chest.

Everyone in prison knows that the way to do maximum damage with a knife is to make as many entry wounds as possible. But before Small could get in a second blow, I came forward, yanking Chase backward by the belt, and rolling him and myself behind the safety cage, which I kicked shut, locking Small in the shower area and protecting us at the same time. Soon as I saw the cage was shut, I blew my whistle. Chase was bent over, blood seeping through his uniform. His instincts had saved him. Sensing what Small was about to do, Chase had managed to turn sideways, deflecting the blade.

Seeing guards arriving to help Chase, I turned my attention to Small. In the brief time since the stabbing, he had already broken down the weapon and managed to shove the pieces into the drain on the shower floor. Two minutes, at most, had passed—yet if a video had been made of the incident and then run in slow-motion, everything would have been clear. In prison, everything happens fast. Things will appear to be functioning smoothly. Everything is happening according to the rules ... then everything changes in an instant. Like the saying, "you never hear the bullet that kills you." In prison, you rarely see the knife that stabs you. Chase did, and that's why he was still alive.

Seeing that Chase was being tended to and that I was okay, other officers moved to immobilize Small. But he was crafty, knowing that as long as his hands were free, he was going to get his ass kicked for hurting an officer. As quick as he could, he got up. "Cuffing up," he cried, backing up to let an officer put handcuffs on him. Even though he would be moved into one of the isolation cells at the end of the Adjustment Center, the escorting officers made sure he would have an accident and "slip on the stairs" on the way there, even though there were no stairs. He couldn't be allowed to stab an officer without payback from the other officers.

Five minutes after Small was led away, I started shaking. It was as though my body was waiting for the threat to be removed before reacting to what had happened.

Counselors showed up and started peppering me with questions: What was Small doing before being taken from his cell? Did he have any grudge against Chase? Did something happen on the way to the showers? No, no, no. I knew that there was no specific reason why he had stabbed Chase. Maybe it was because Small was in a bad mood, or because he felt it was time to get an officer, or maybe he was just tired of the noise on his unit and wanted to go off to a quiet cell for a while. Maybe Small himself didn't even know why he had almost killed a correctional officer.

Chase's stabbing seemed to set the day on edge. Even if inmates don't immediately know what has happened on the other side of the prison, even within their housing unit, they quickly find out. Two hours later, still morning, another officer and I were getting ready to take an inmate from the Adjustment Center to the hospital. We'd thoroughly searched him and had already started moving him. All of a sudden, we heard shots and whistles. We immediately knew that a fight had broken out and the prison was being shut down—meaning all movement of prisoners stopped. We put the inmate we were escorting into a holding cell and then went to the gate for orders.

In the South Yard, at least seventy-five inmates were flush against the wall, hands in the air—with gunmen poised above them, rifles at the ready. In the middle of the exercise area, a white inmate was trying to get up to make it to the exit gate. The assailants had waited for the victim to start lifting weights. Then, when he was pumping iron, two men ran up, grabbing the bar and pressing it against his throat, while another two men came up to knife him in the throat and crotch. Like with all prison stabbings, it was over before anyone else saw what had happened.

Now blood was spurting from his neck and groin.

"Fall, motherfucker," a black inmate shouted.

"Yeah, go down, bitch," a second yelled.

The wounded man wobbled and veered toward us, trying to stay on his feet long enough to get off the yard. Another white inmate broke forward to help him. In an instant, a guard fired two loads of birdshot into the dirt at his feet, stopping him in his tracks. Everyone, officers and inmates, watched the bleeding inmate stumble and continue on toward us. He had to make it off the yard without help, or he would have been considered a "bitch" and a coward. He had to show he had guts. No officer moved to assist him. They would have been signing his death warrant—so we watched the man veer toward the gate, all the while his blue shirt and pants turning red.

"Can't we go get him, sergeant?" a new officer asked.

"Hell, no," said Sergeant Finley. "He's gotta come to us."

The blood loss must have weakened him. He slumped against a screen ten yards from where a stretcher had already been brought to carry him to the hospital. If he had gone down, the staff would have had to get him … but they didn't want to go against the law of the yard … unless there was nothing else to do. Somehow he found the strength to continue, and he wavered on toward us. Finally, Sergeant Finley opened the gate and let him drop onto the stretcher rolled up beside us. The situation now under control, my partner and I were told to go back and continue escorting to the hospital the inmate we had been with when the stabbing occurred in the yard. I guess I was still thinking about the other inmate who had just been stabbed when I got back to the holding cell. I glanced in at the inmate, saw that his hands were still cuffed behind his back, and I unlocked the cell.

Like a kid skipping rope, he jumped up in the air and in one instant got his hands in front of his body, yanked a knife from under his belt, and struck me in the chest. Now I was the one wounded. As I staggered back, my partner grabbed the knife, knocked the inmate back inside the door, and then pulled me out of the cell, slamming the door just as I had done two hours earlier with Chase. Unlike him, there was no blood coming through my uniform where the blade had slashed the shirt.

I stuck my hand into my chest pocket and pulled out a plastic mirror I always carried to be able to see around darkened corners for someone waiting in ambush or to stick under bunks to spot hidden weapons. It wasn't much good now. Across the surface was a long scratch, which on my face would have given me a scar ear-to-ear.

Two stabbings and one attempted stabbing and it wasn't even noon.

The inmates must have wanted to set a prison record that day, for at three o'clock an inmate stumbled and fell in one of the Adjustment Center yards. His stab wounds were too serious to be treated at the prison hospital, so he was transferred to Marin General, where he later died. No weapon was ever recovered and no attacker was ever seen. It was as though the knife just came out of nowhere all by itself, cut the man up, and then disappeared.

That night I went straight to Zimm's restaurant to forget the stabbings I had seen and the close call I myself had had. It wasn't until another guard said he'd better give me a ride that I finally went home. Fortunately, Amy was asleep … or pretending to be asleep. I fell on the bed in my uniform, clutching my little friend—the plastic mirror.

I used to think, if I'm a cat, how many lives do I have left? The thought chilled me: What if there was only one to start with? A week later I was on an Extraction Team in the North Block getting ready to remove an inmate from the cell he refused to leave. Usually an officer will be present with a video camera to film the extraction, just in case the inmate says he was brutalized during the extraction; there will be proof he wasn't. Well, he could have been, but it was hard to see clearly with everything that was going on. Besides, the backs of the Extraction Team members sometimes prevent the viewer from seeing what really happened. Real TV would have paid millions to show what we filmed with the Extraction Team. It's not hard to imagine: One man doesn't want to leave a space. Five other men insist he does. The image speaks for itself.

This particular day there was no officer carrying a video camera. The sergeant outlined who the inmate was and his history at the institution. "Take him down," he said, giving us the code term that told us the inmate was a real trouble-maker and that we should kick his ass to teach him a lesson. Issued with inverted, U-shaped shields and helmets, we went up to get him. Maybe because I was sort of stout then, the other officers had me in the lead. They were going to open the cell, thrust me on the inmate, and then rush in to immobilize him. The trouble was the inmate knew we were coming. He had yanked off his mattress and was using it for protection, while he taunted us to come and get him.

To be honest, I had a hangover that morning and knew the extraction was going to be a tough one. I glanced around as the gunman came up the railing, racking up his shotgun, getting ready to fire if something bad happened. Seeing the gunman, the inmate crouched down behind the mattress—trying to make himself less of a target.

"Ready, Woolf?" another officer asked me.

"Fuck it! Let's not mess with this asshole. Just shoot him." I winked at the officer, a gesture the inmate didn't catch.

"But we're supposed to go in and get him," someone said.

"Fuck it. Let's just shoot him and say he went for me with a knife."

"But you know how much paperwork it is killing an inmate," said another officer.

"Beats getting my uniform dirty."

Now the inmate was hearing this conversation and lowered the mattress to get a better look at what was going on.

I stepped back and motioned to the gunman. "Shoot this motherfucker, but hit him in the head. I don't want those slugs ricocheting onto us."

The gunman was new ... and I could tell he was nervous, but he lifted the shotgun and aimed it at the terrified inmate.

"What d'ya think you're doin'?" yelled the inmate. "I ain't got no knife."

"Then drop the mattress and cuff-up so we can see," I ordered.

Two minutes later, we had him out of the cell without any difficulty.

One of the officers slapped me on the back. "Nice bluff, Woolf, but what if the gunman had killed him?"

"'If' is like another planet. I've never been there."

Being a guard, you win one, you lose one. You're like an accountant with a ledger for yourself. You try to keep everything in the black and out of the red. But no matter how hard you try, you know that red's going to turn up when you least expect it.

Months later, I was coming down a tier when burning liquid was thrown into my face. I yelled in pain, trying to get the sticky solution off my face. Just then I felt a jab in my leg and knew I had been shot by a poison dart.

Sure enough. Twenty minutes later while a nurse was dabbing an antibiotic solution on my burned face, a doctor was working to remove a sliver of metal from my skin. An inmate I hardly had dealings with had used his stinger, an electrical coil used to heat coffee and soup, to cook up a cup of his urine. When he had it boiling, he added his own feces, stirring it until it became a paste. Then he added sugar to make sure the urine would stick to the skin of his victim, blistering it, giving the poison more time to start an infection in the wound made by the home-made dart dipped in the mixture.

When he had his concoction ready, he sat back and waited for his unsuspecting target to pass. Chance decided it would be me.

I always paid attention, but it was never enough. I only had one set of eyes. Inmates were like some mythical beast with hundreds of them, eyes that could see around corners before you came into view walking along, thinking about lunch or about having a drink after work. Then everything would come down on you, as if the prison were a jealous lover who didn't want you to think about anything else. I soon learned not to. Sooner or later, I knew that I was going to experience a riot. It wasn't just that every Hollywood prison movie I could remember always had a riot scene. Sometimes I would talk to the old-timers about past riots at San Quentin. I just figured odds were that a riot would happen … one day or another.

When it finally came, I got more than I ever imagined. I didn't just witness it; I was an active participant … even though all I did was flee for my life. If I've ever aged rapidly, it was that morning. I was a young man walking out on the yard and an older one leaving it.

It was a planned, armed confrontation in the Upper Yard among the blacks, whites, and Hispanics. Thirty-one shots were fired to control the situation. Forty-two stabbing instruments were seized. One inmate died of his injuries. A second received birdshot in his eye. More than one hundred inmates were treated for knife and birdshot wounds. Two correctional officers were also wounded, one with numerous shotgun wounds to his leg. The warden declared a general emergency and ordered the prison locked down.

Before, all the confrontations I had seen were one-on-one. Now there were over twelve hundred men fighting each other in an area half the size of a footfall field.

It all started with one incident, nothing really, one inmate pushing another. Then a punch was thrown, and suddenly, like an igniting flash-point, scores of men began fighting. Before I knew it, scores of inmates were facing off, with knives and picks materializing from under their shirts.

Boom! Boom! Boom! sounded from the wall. Gunmen were firing buckshot in front of inmates, having it ricochet up to sting and not maim them. Then whistles cut through the air around me.

I froze.

All around me three huge racial groups were going after each other. I don't remember thinking. I just started walking as fast as my thick legs would carry me to the gate—where other officers were forming up. If I ran, I knew I would be dead. I wouldn't see where I was going, and I'd either be shot or stabbed. I moved like a guy with a bad case of *turista* who has to find a toilet, fast.

The inmates weren't after me. But if I got in the way of a blade, no one was going to hold off until I passed. I was going to get stabbed, too. As I was striding though the melee, I saw birdshot spraying up, convicts stabbing each other, and people rolling on the ground. The gate seemed like it was receding farther and father away.

I was one big heartbeat thumping inside my chest. I kept glancing up at the walkways, trying to see where the gunmen were.

"Woolf!" a guard called, motioning with his rifle barrel toward an area beyond the yellow dead line where guards were grouped under the protection of three gunmen.

Then, snap, as though an unheard signal were given, everyone stopped fighting. I mean, in an instant. It was as though they had been struck with a debilitating illness that stripped away their strength in an instant. They began dropping their knives, pipes, and razor blades. Then they lowered to the ground. What twenty seconds before had been a thousand men fighting became wave after wave of motionless figures stretching out on their stomachs. They must have known the emergency response button had been pushed, and telephone numbers were automatically being called at the home of every guard not on duty. All over Marin County, police, sheriffs, and highway patrol officers were on the way. If things had gotten worse, then the National Guard would have been called in, too. But none of the other law enforcement groups were allowed inside the walls. Only the correctional staff would be allowed inside to deal with the riot.

Scores of officers were forming up at the gate and being issued rifles and shotguns. As they moved past the gate, a captain tapped each on the shoulder, giving him his assignment: "Gun Rail! Gun Rail! Yard! Yard!"

I looked at my watch. Twenty minutes had passed since the first whistle blew. My shirt was drenched with sweat, but I hadn't been touched.

When the first of the massive Civil War steel doors clanked shut behind me, I knew I had survived. The Department of Corrections doesn't issue medals for riots the way the armed forces does for campaigns. But I awarded myself The Scared Shitless Award. Helping me to move through the riot was the realization that the prison had a no-hostage policy. If an inmate grabbed me to use me to get out, I was doomed. All I had to do was remember Attica, and what happened to those guards. Ever since George Jackson and his accomplices took over the Adjustment Center and killed their guards, the prison has refused to trade lives for freedom. Whenever I wasn't inside the walls, their policy made sense, but not when I was walking the tiers. I wanted to convince myself that the warden would have made an exception for me. After all, I was Rudy J. Woolf.

The thought made me laugh. I would be mowed down with the rest.

-#-

15

Visiting Daze

What happened later the same Easter Day I encountered the frightened boy see-ing his father yanked me from my memories and thrust me back into my role as correctional officer at San Quentin. In an instant, I saw why I could never take things for granted. No matter how innocent the setting, someone was preparing to destroy it. In prison, nothing is "just" what it seems. Even silence has to be interpreted differently—as far as where it occurs, when it occurs, and how long it lasts. Whether in a far-flung corner of the prison, the yard, a cell, or a work area, a plan is always being devised. For a correctional officer, the secret is to discover what might happen before it does.

That day, as I was monitoring the Visiting Room, a young black woman came in.

She was carrying what had to be about a six-month-old baby girl. The woman had been checked and cleared to enter the Visiting Room. Sitting down at a vacant table with the baby, she put a diaper bag down in front of her and bottle of formula to the side. Then she seemed to relax, as though trying to get ready for a visit with her boyfriend.

It was a little after two, about an hour after visiting time had started. Moving through the room, I glanced over at the little boy who had been so frightened when he had first arrived. Now, he was leaning forward, smiling, and talking to his father. When I passed back by the woman with the baby, I noticed that she was bottle-feeding her with chocolate milk.

It seemed the most innocent, natural thing in the world—a mother feeding a baby with a bottle—yet it did seem strange that the baby should have been bot-tle-fed at such an early age. And what kind of mother would give her infant choc-olate milk? I wondered as I continued around the room.

A few minutes later, the boyfriend was brought and sat down at the woman's table. They settled right in to chatting and looking at the baby—all the while the mother was feeding the baby the chocolate milk.

About twenty minutes later, the woman got up and, setting the baby on the table, started to change its diaper. She took off the soiled diaper, wiped off the baby's bottom, and started to put on a change of diapers. But her behavior changed. It was such a subtle difference that I don't think it would have shown up on film—between the moment before she started changing the diaper and the moment after. Yet I saw the change, a certain nervousness on the mother's part, glancing around, as though there was something wrong about changing a baby's diaper. I started over toward her. As I got closer, I could see that the contents of the diaper were unusually runny, and they were emitting a strong odor different from that of soiled diapers.

Now the boyfriend started looking around, fidgeting and playing with his dreadlocks while his girlfriend went on changing the diaper. Then, picking up the soiled diaper, he started toward the trash can by the restroom door. At that moment I focused on the inmate. Reaching the trash, he took something from the diaper and swallowed it.

I couldn't believe it. I stopped for a second, stunned by what he had done, and trying to make sense of it to myself. Another officer had also seen what the inmate had done and was converging on him at the same time. We immediately grabbed him. I tried to get my finger inside his mouth, trying to get him to spit out what he had swallowed. But he was resisting us, locking his teeth and trying to keep me from forcing his mouth open.

Within moments, there were five of us struggling with the inmate to restrain him. We got him to the floor, struggling to get him to cough out what he had swallowed. But it was too late. He had already gotten it down. The inmate was rushed to the prison hospital to have his stomach x-rayed. As I got up, I glanced across the room.

As long as I live I'll remember the face of the little boy staring in horror at us. And it didn't take a second to realize what he was seeing: five huge guards beating up a man just for trying to empty a diaper into the trash. All the trust I had built up with him that morning was gone in an instant.

I looked away and went back to monitoring the Visiting Room until closing time.

As I came off the overtime shift, the lieutenant told me the inmate had been found with eight balloons of heroin in his stomach. It didn't take long before we learned that the inmate's girlfriend had fed the balloons to the baby before coming to San Quentin. She had coated the balloons with Vaseline so they could slide easily down the baby's narrow esophagus. The chocolate liquid wasn't milk but ex-lax.

The mother had planned for there to be enough time to get the balloons into the baby, then go to the Visiting Room and feed her the laxative which, with her small size, quickly would pass through her intestinal tract and carry out the balloons, which the boy friend planned to swallow before returning to his cell—where he would induce himself to vomit up the balloons of heroin, which he could then cut up and sell. A horrible little plan with the baby at its center.

When I realized what the mother and boyfriend had done to the baby, I was sickened. It was the most disgusting thing I had ever seen in years of witnessing what I had thought were the worst things one inmate could do to another—but here was a mother ready to let her baby die smuggling drugs into prison.

I couldn't shake it from my mind: like an unbroken line of pain with the terrified boy at one end and the baby filled with heroin at the other. What had they done? Nothing. They were merely children.

Now the damage was done. Because of a heartless, illegal, and dangerous act, the quartet in the Visiting Room—the little boy, the baby, the girlfriend and the inmate—would never be the same.

The mother who fed balloons of heroin to her child would be charged with drug smuggling and reckless child endangerment. She would almost certainly have her child taken away from her. Her only chance to keep her would be to name names and reveal all the identities involved in who procured the heroin for her. Of course, with a strong chance that gang affiliation was involved, the woman would have to choose between keeping her mouth shut and losing her baby, or giving up the people she got the drugs from—and risk being killed as a snitch. A tough choice for any mother to make.

As for the inmate who tried to swallow the balloons, after he had his stomach x-rayed, he would be placed in an Enforcement Cell, an empty, windowless room with no toilet. Inmates have to urinate in one bucket and defecate in another. Once he finished, the door would open and a guard would take the feces and urine to a medical technician, who would go through the fecal matter to make certain all the balloons shown on the X-ray had been eliminated from the inmate's stomach. If not, then the inmate would be kept inside the Enforcement Cell as long as it took for the heroin-filled balloons to pass.

The inmate had better hope to God he could defecate them, for sooner or later the acid in the stomach will eat through the rubber and the heroin will explode in his system, killing him from a overdose.

Some correctional officers took bets on whether he would get the balloons out in time. A few wanted to see the balloons burst inside the inmate, not just because he had tried to get drugs past us, and his death would make one less prick to deal with—but because he had been willing to risk his own daughter to smuggle heroin past the walls.

If he survived the Enforcement Room, the inmate would be taken to Administrative Housing. All his visits and privileges would be cancelled. He would wait to be interviewed by a counselor investigating all aspects of how the heroin was brought into San Quentin: The inmate stood a strong chance of having his sentence extended.

But the stiffest punishment was reserved for the baby. She might never learn how close she had come to dying had one of the balloons burst in her stomach. She might grow up as an adopted child and never know who her true mother was.

As for her father, she might not ever learn he was a prisoner in a maximum prison. Worst of all, she might never know how little her life meant to him. Maybe it would be better that she never learned anything of what happened in the Visiting Room. Maybe it was best that she never got to know her father.

I certainly got to know mine.

The little boy was the one person I didn't want to think about. I sensed the pain he would now carry. I only hoped it would not lead him inside prison walls in either uniform: his father's or mine.

-#-

16

Blood Lines

Some people clutch to their families all their lives. Others pull away and try to forget where and who they come from. That's what I tried to do. But my father and Griff kept surfacing to cause trouble, as though they were always moving parallel to me—always out of sight, yet ready at a moment's notice to appear before me, blocking my path, putting a new crisis in my way.

"You can't get rid of us," they seemed to be saying in unison.

I gave up hoping they would go away. Griff and my father together were like reflections in a fun house mirror. My father never seemed to change with time, while Griff appeared to have absorbed every blow that came his way. Griff was scared and battered. The effects of drugs and booze erupted in his jumpy movements and were etched across his drawn face.

He looked and acted like a prematurely aged, punch-drunk fighter.

My father was still volcanic with energy. Nothing fazed him. He was a slab of marble that didn't crack or chip, whereas Griff was a chunk of clay that crumbled at the slightest touch. Over the past several years, they had taken turns going to prison.

Stopped by the police for running a red light in Santa Barbara, my father gave the police officer a different license than he had given him two weeks before when he had been pulled over for speeding in the same city.

After arresting him for using a license under a fictitious name, police searched the boat he was living on and found thirty-seven drivers' licenses, each with a different name; and all with social security cards and credit cards to match the names on the licenses.

Combining the limit on all the bogus cards, my father had over a million dollars in credit. This time, even with his friends who were judges and local politicians, he couldn't get the charges dismissed. He was going to do time—and not just in jail or at a work farm. Because of previous convictions, my father was sentenced to Soledad for multiple counts of identity theft. As soon as he got off the bus with the other arriving inmates, a lieutenant started roll call. He called out one name after another ... then said, "Rudy Woolf."

"Here," my father said.

"You any relation to another Rudy Woolf?"

"He's my son."

The lieutenant told another officer giving the roll call to take the others to reception, then motioned my father aside.

Within a week, my father was working as a typist in the captain's office. It was the same as letting a wolf into the fold. Later, he bragged he made more money behind the bars than he did on the outside. Like everything he said or did, it was an exaggeration—but he had figured out how to make money while an inmate.

From what I learned later, his business started with an inmate talking about how his wife couldn't get a car without credit. Because he was a trustee in the office, my father was able to make a phone call outside, to a friend of his who had a used car business. Once that detail was worked out, he called another friend who had a finance business.

The next day the inmate's daughter went into the car lot of my father's friend, picked out a car she liked, and then was referred by the salesman to a loan company that would be able to cover a car loan. All she needed was the down payment. Because she didn't have the money for the down payment, my father's friend steered her to yet another finance company to get a personal loan. Soon she was paying thirty percent interest, and my father was getting a cut from the car agency and both loan companies.

He was off and running.

Within a few months, the inmate who had first approached my father came up, saying that his girlfriend hadn't been able to keep up the payments and the car had been repossessed. My father expressed his sympathy but said it wasn't his fault. But by then he had already picked up a cut from the car being repossessed. He was soon selling a dozen cars a month through the same method. He was making so much money that he realized he couldn't have it coming to him at the prison. Kelly was selected to be the company banker, and following my father's advice always to deal in cash, she opened a safe-deposit box and started stashing money inside.

My father was doing so well that salesmen were calling him to ask him his secret. They were walking around lots, selling only four or five cars a month, and my father was in prison, selling twice as many. It wasn't long until a guard heard about my father's skill at helping people without funds to get a used car. My father was glad to oblige.

Guards may rule the prisons, but inmates control them.

With a true entrepreneur's spirit, my father decided to expand his business, so he started getting involved in the inmates' conjugal visits. For a little kickback he would make sure an inmate's name was on the right list and, for another little sign of gratitude, that the inmate's name moved up higher, bumping others lower down. Some inmates wanted weekly visits, and my father was only too willing to help out. "Nothing more important than the family," he said … and they believed him. They should have; he was telling the truth … they just didn't know what kind of family he meant.

As for Griff, he didn't do as well as our father. He'd been making money, too, but a lot less than my father in prison. Then Griff got busted for making bombs and dealing drugs.

I couldn't believe my brother could be calm enough to mix explosives. Visiting him before trial, I asked how he ever learned to make a bomb.

"Nothing to it, man. It's real simple. You just take a lot of gun powder and jam it down this thing, then you run a fuse down the pipe, and you got yourself a bomb that can blow up this whole fuckin' jail."

Luckily for Griff, his charges were reduced to burglary. Still, he drew four years at Pleasant Valley.

The imprisonments of my father and Griff were always staggered. It was as though they had made an unspoken vow never to be in prison at the same time—like a weird form of hide-and-seek, where one of them had to be on the outside to wait his turn for the other to leave prison, so he himself could go back in. But this time both were behind bars—and, in a way, so was I. Even though they would never have been allowed to serve out their time in a prison where I was a working as a correctional officer, I had missed encountering both of them at San Quentin, being off at Folsom when my father passed through on his way somewhere else, and working on a transportation unit at Soledad when Griff spent three weeks inside the San Quentin Reception Center.

Our only reunion behind bars was when I went as a family member to visit my father in jail or to pick Griff up upon his release from prison.

I suppose there are stranger places for family to meet … although I can't think of many.

-#-

17

Pleasant Valley

All sorts of places can qualify for the "middle of nowhere." Pleasant Valley is one. The name must have been the practical joke by whoever first went there expecting to find grass hillsides, groves of trees swaying in the wind, and maybe even a quiet river meandering through the landscape. Nothing further from the truth. It would have been more accurate to call it Unpleasant Valley, for one of the state's medium security prisons was located smack in the middle of unbroken cattle country. Pleasant Valley resembled the sort of place you would never go unless you had been sent there to do time as an inmate or serve as a correctional officer … which are almost the same thing.

Griff had been there two years and was coming up on his parole hearing.

Being a guard at another Department of Corrections prison, I wasn't allowed to visit my brother in my capacity as a law enforcement officer, but I could see him on visiting days as other families did. Twice I drove down monotonous Highway 5 to see Griff. The most boring drive of my life … the same damned religious nuts ranting on the radio, the same fast food restaurants and gas stations.

At Pleasant Valley, Griff wasn't doing well: The San Joaquin Valley heat was getting to him, and he said the Mexican gangs were making it hell for the whites inside. It was an open housing with Level II Security, which meant there was a lot of freedom for the prison population to move around; there was also a lot of gang movement and violence. Griff had to pay attention—something that all the amphetamine he'd taken made it hard for him to do.

During my calls and visits, I told him to "do his own time," and to keep away from any gang enticements. If anyone offered him a cigarette, candy bar, or joint, he was to turn it down—for once he accepted something, no matter how insignificant, people would have their hooks in him.

When Griff first got to Pleasant Valley, I had made a few calls to officers I knew from San Quentin who had transferred down there. I asked them to keep an eye out for my brother. They would do it for me just as I would for any relative of a fellow correctional officer turning up at San Quentin. They took Griff aside and asked, "Do you have a brother working at San Quentin?"

Soon as he answered "yes," the staff tried to get him a cushy job out of harm's way. They weren't just trying to make points with me; it was respect for a fellow correctional officer. They knew Pleasant Valley had inmates who had been at San Quentin, too. Some of them might have had a grudge against me, and if they'd learned my little brother was serving time there it wouldn't have been long before Griff got stabbed in the yard or was found dead in the shower one morning. If the inmates want get to you, they will.

Staying by himself, Griff would be okay ... unless there was going to be a prison-wide racial fight. Then he would have to fallout in the yard with the whites and fight like a gladiator with them—or be killed for disloyalty.

It wasn't easy for him. Griff said that Pleasant Valley was as tough as San Quentin in many ways. "There are so many stabbings here. It's not safe. Yesterday, they blew the whistle and I dropped down like everybody else, and a guard on the tower fired right over my head, and blew the leg off the guy I had been talking to behind me. Man, I was just praying I'd get through the day."

I told him I'd try to get down for another visit, but my life was stretched like a rubber band ready to snap. Every week, though, I would telephone to see how he was doing. He told me he was x-ing off the days till his release. This was a bad sign, for it meant he was working against time, instead of flowing with it, accepting where he was ... until the prison coffin opened and he was free. The two years and a half years that passed fast for me were an endless 910 days and nights for Griff.

One summer afternoon while working on the East Block at San Quentin, I received a call from a captain I knew at Pleasant Valley. Griff was going to be released early, in two weeks, and the officer wanted to know if I wanted to come get him. If I drove down, he'd cut Griff loose early. If I didn't go get him, Griff would have to spend two more days working his way through the discharge process. The captain was doing me a big favor. Besides, once he did get out, it didn't seem fair for Griff to have to take a Greyhound all the way up to Marin County.

I thanked the captain but told him I couldn't get down until after work. "Just tell Griff to sit tight. I'll be down soon as I can tonight."

"Take your time," the Captain laughed. "He's not going anywhere until you get here."

I ran into heavy traffic all the way from the Richmond—San Rafael Bridge to Highway 5. Once I got on the interstate, though, I made good time—stopping only to gas up, take a piss, and gulp down coffee.

All this time Griff was sitting in a chair in the captain's office, with all his belongings beside him in two cardboard boxes. For Griff to sit still twelve minutes, let alone twelve hours, would have required all the focus he had. But sit was all he could do. He wasn't allowed to go outside for a cigarette or a snack. Food had to be brought in to him, and whenever he had to go to the bathroom, two escorts had to accompany him.

I later heard that within an hour he was a mass of twitches and jerks. I didn't know it at the time, and even if I had, I couldn't drive any faster than I did. Still, I didn't get to the prison entrance until one in the morning. All the administration offices were darkened. I walked over to the guard post by the first gate and told the sergeant on duty I had come to get my brother, Griff Woolf.

"We don't release inmates at night. Come back in the daytime."

"The captain knows I'm coming."

"What the hell are you talking about?" said the sergeant, the veins on his neck bulging.

I could tell he was angry that some asshole was showing up, trying to create work for him, when he wanted to listen to the music I could hear softly coming from the radio he had probably turned down when he saw my headlights in the parking lot.

"Check with the captain. You'll see."

Snorting, the sergeant went back in the shack and made a phone call. A minute later he returned. "Wait here," he said.

Minutes passed. Then I saw a gunman come out of a turret and move up against the railing, holding his rifle at port arms. Moments later, the main gate swung open. Caught in a spotlight brighter than the lights on the walls, Griff emerged, flanked by four guards, two of them carrying his possessions.

The sergeant at the gate was livid. He had never seen an inmate released at night.

"Let's get the fuck out of here," Griff said as we climbed into the car.

I pulled into the first gas station we came to, went inside, and bought a rose inside a plastic vial sold at the counter.

When I got back into the car, Griff was staring at me with a weird expression. He must have thought I'd bought the rose for him. Putting the flower on the dashboard, I started the engine, pulled out of the gas station, did a U-turn, and started back toward where we had come from.

"Where you going?"

"Back to the prison."

"Are you crazy?" Griff shouted, flapping his arms around like an angry seagull. "Fuck, I just did two years in that motherfucker and you're taking me back?"

Five minutes later I pulled into the parking lot and turned off the engine, being sure to take the keys so Griff wouldn't steal the car. Taking the rose, I got out.

Griff leaned over in the seat. "Where the fuck are you going with that?"

"Watch!"

I walked back to the guard station at the entrance. The same officer was on duty. Seeing me coming with my hands behind my back, he rose up, his hand going down to his holster. As I got closer, I held out the rose. "Here, have a nice day."

His mouth dropped open.

Not giving him a chance to speak, I turned around and walked back to the car, from where Griff had seen everything. He didn't say anything until we were on Highway 5 heading north. "Hey, man, are you queer now?"

I reached over and stroked his cheek, and tried to make my voice sound as high-pitched as I could. "Didn't dad tell you?"

Then I laughed.

So did Griff, eventually.

-#-

18

Riding Shotgun

Today there's a cap on the number of hours a correctional officer can work over-time. But when I was at San Quentin, some of us were putting in the equivalent of ninety-six hours of work weekly, month after month. Along with daily over-time, we were selling our credited time off and our vacations, too, then doubling up on our days off and getting paid for back-to-back shifts. I was earning big money. I was making more than the warden. Hell, I was making more money than the governor of California. But I was paying for it in return—and so was Amy. I kept saying I was making all the money for my family, but it was a cop out. Except for sleeping, I was hardly home when not working. I was drinking and taking drugs to relax. The more I worked, the more I needed to unwind, and the more I unwound the more drugs and alcohol flowed through me.

Being at San Quentin isn't like working in an office building. In business, you figure on going home after work. In prison, you can never be sure whether you'll be coming out of the walls on your own or on a gurney or zipped inside a body bag. Working inside a prison is like playing cat-and-mouse inside a maze. You may think you're the cat, but at any moment you can become the mouse. At a max-A prison, nothing is for certain except uncertainty.

There's a constant risk that translates into the body producing adrenaline, and adrenaline is addictive, a high the body produces on its own. You become your own dealer and user, stressing out so you can feel the rush. I heard that the enamel on the backs of the teeth of gamblers, test pilots, and big game hunters is eroded away because of constant adrenaline. I believe it. My dentist said the enamel on my teeth looks like it's been ground down by a Brillo pad.

For all its risks, prison had one asset missing from the business world. Prison was never boring. No matter where I found myself inside the walls—whether in the hospital, the church, the carpentry shops, and especially walking the tiers—I never knew for sure if my next step was my last. Staying alert was my top priority. But eventually, when I was working double shifts day after day, night after night, my body started coming down. It couldn't maintain constant vigil without assistance, and that's where the speed and cocaine came in. They revved me back up for a while ... until I crashed. Burned-out from coming off a double shift, I would leave San Quentin, stop for a few drinks or a couple of snorts, and then go home.

When I walked in the door, if I was still walking and not stumbling, there would be less-than-nothing of me left to be a husband, to be a father, even to be a human being. All I wanted to do was pass out until the next morning when I could get up and go back to do it again.

Amy showed as much patience as any wife trying to hold on to a disintegrating marriage. But then finally she let go. For the second time in our marriage, she applied for a divorce. "This time there's no turning back," she said. No burning the divorce papers when I made things better. The only thing going up in flames now was our marriage.

In the midst of breaking up, we realized that a legal divorce would make her situation worse. Doctors finally were able to tell her that her problem wasn't in just in her imagination. Progress had been made into the disorder she and countless other women were suffering from. She was diagnosed as having bulimia and anorexia. Devastating conditions in their own right, they also worked to throw off her electrolytes, affecting her blood pressure and impairing her thinking.

The more she told me about her condition, the more I realized it was beyond her control. Of course, I had added to her stress, but now she could get help ... if she continued to be covered by my correctional officer's benefits. If she divorced me, she would lose all her medical insurance, and even though the women in the group she had been attending kept urging her to sign the papers and be done with me, she held off. God knows, there was reason enough not to.

Even though I had sworn never to do to Amy or the children what my father had done to my mother, my siblings, and me—use physical violence—I knew there were many ways of hitting someone emotionally, and I was guilty of many even though I never raised my hand. All Amy had ever asked of me was to be <u>there</u> for her; and all I had done in response was to be elsewhere more and more of the time.

Now, along with my drinking I was doing drugs: uppers to keep me going, cocaine to help me relax, and downers to help me crash.

I was taking more illegal drugs than she was prescription ones.

Doing no good for her, Gail, or Brian, I moved out.

I couldn't have gone to a worse place than back to my father's. I don't even know why I did. I suppose I thought I was stronger. I would be in charge of the situation. And I think maybe I was hoping to change things from my childhood, to make it right once I got back at home with my father, just once. Instead, it provided him with the perfect opportunity for him to tell me how right he had been about Amy being "a worthless bitch."

As soon as I walked in the door, he started up with the same question he had been hammering me with years: "Why did you betray the family by marrying that bitch?"

When I was a boy, listening to my father's ranting was like being in a room with a horrible record that I couldn't stop playing—but now I could, no matter how bad my life was. I realized it would only get worse if I didn't get out, and I couldn't wait to. The apartment studio I rented wasn't much larger than the room I had lived in after leaving my father. Now I was older, but not wiser because I had left my wife and child.

I couldn't ask for help at San Quentin. If I told my supervisors at work I had a substance abuse problem, I would have been put on medical leave and have lost all my overtime. So I rode it out, whatever it was I was going through. And I knew that there was always San Quentin to jack me back up, with its dank tiers and surly stares. Things could be worse.

Working sixteen hours a day took my mind off everything. Routine made me its slave. San Quentin was like a sanctuary where I could hide from the responsibilities of my life. And if one of the sergeants and lieutenants sensed that I was edgy or sullenly working my way through a hangover, they said nothing. They had enough problems of their own; even if they didn't, they still knew they could count on Woolf.

The apartment I rented became like a waiting room for going back to work at San Quentin, and with nothing to do while waiting, I got more and more stoned. The come-down from cocaine was bad enough, but the let-down from speed was like falling off a ladder over and over again and always landing on my head. I started worrying that some of the inmates knew I was getting stoned before work and had told their buddies on the outside.

I started leaving my snub-nosed .38 on the table while I snorted coke. I wanted to be ready when they came through the door. One afternoon the door swung open, and I grabbed the gun and fired twice, miraculously missing the figure in the doorway and sending the bullets past him. It was Griff. In spite of all the close calls he had been through, my brother still was flooded with fear. "What the fuck you trying to do, kill me?"

I knew it wouldn't make sense if I said "no." I apologized and with all the breath I had left, I blew the cocaine dust off the table onto the floor.

Griff's face dropped. "Why the fuck did you do that, man?"

I dropped my head. "I could have murdered my own brother and ended up on Death Row at San Quentin."

"But you didn't."

"Didn't" didn't count. I had snorted my last line of coke and dropped my last speedball. I was so dirty there was nothing left but to either clean up or point the .38 at myself.

-#-

19

Cut Ups

Later, I thought it must have been like the blind leading the blind, although the elderly black inmate really couldn't see. I drove him over alone on Christmas Day to San Francisco General Hospital because the hospital at San Quentin couldn't diagnose his deteriorating condition. The Department of Corrections farms out patients to different medical facilities in the area and it was San Francisco General's turn to treat our inmates. I watched a nurse get the old inmate settled in a room. Then I pulled up a chair outside his room and started waiting to be relieved. The secured ward at the hospital was like any other containment area—except for the medical equipment in the cells. The ward was monitored from a thick-glass booth inside the entrance. Two correctional officers could see down both sides of the cells, one side of which contained prisoners while the other held psychotic patients. At the far end of the ward was a recreation room, where controlled groups—those who were ambulatory or permitted out of their cells—could watch television. Usually two deputies patrolled the rec room and the hallways, but I didn't see more than one that day. They must have figured Christmas would be quiet, so they could cut down on staff. Let the married deputies stay home with their families.

I knew the routine. Normally two correctional officers would stand guard over a prisoner at the hospital. One, unarmed, would remain in the room with the patient; the other, armed, would sit outside in the hall. The lieutenant who assigned me to transport the old blind man knew he wouldn't be a security risk. Where was he going to go if he couldn't see? And I sensed there wouldn't be any trouble on the ward. As it was Christmas time, nurses were decorating the recreation room.

An orderly brought me a cup of coffee, and I sat sipping it, wondering if I had gotten Amy the right color bathrobe, and if Brian and Gail would like their gifts. Starting to get a little sleepy, I got up to stretch and take a walk down the hall. When I reached the security station, I noticed that instead of the two jailers from the sheriff's department inside, there was only one. Recognizing the sheriff from previous visits, I tapped on the glass. He filled me in on where his partner was. Apparently, there had been a major automobile accident on Mission Street. A drunk driver had killed two people. Seriously injured, the driver had been brought to the hospital, operated on, and then brought up to the jail ward, where he had been placed under arrest by the Highway Patrol but was now being watched by the other sheriff's deputy, who would be back as soon as he could. Normally, the Highway Patrol would be guarding their own prisoners, but all were needed for patrol duty.

I wandered back to the room I was guarding and checked to make sure the blind inmate was doing all right. Then I sat back down. For obvious reasons, correctional officers can't nap on duty; neither can they read magazines or books. They have to wait out the wait, which is what I did. I was used to filling in blank time up on the guard towers. Besides, having arrived at 7:20 in the morning, I knew that I would be relieved at three, with plenty of time on Christmas Day to be with Amy, Gail, and Brian. Amy and I had decided to make a "fresh start" of our marriage … and I was going to make certain I did all I could to be a good husband and father.

At about 2:30 p.m., I got a phone call from a lieutenant at San Quentin. "Hey, Woolf, would you mind working an additional eight-hour shift?" he asked.

I was kinda hesitant to accept. Then I figured, what the hell, I was already there on overtime working on a holiday. Now I'd have double overtime.

I knew Amy was gonna be mad and the kids were going to be disappointed—but I tried to convince myself that the extra money would make it right. So I settled into my second shift. The way my chair was positioned I could see the entire hallway, both in the direction of the recreation room and toward the security booth, with a nurse's station in the middle. At about five-thirty I noticed several inmates wandering around in hospital gowns. It bothered me to see people who were supposed to be either locked up or monitored walking around without escorts. When the next nurse passed, I asked her what was going on.

"We decided we wanted to do something together this year. We're going to let all the people in the jail ward celebrate Christmas together and have a nice time."

As soon as I heard her response, I got nervous. One of the rules I had learned early on was never to mix inmates unless you were certain that there were no gang conflicts or paybacks coming from one person to another. It's like a chemistry set. You don't go pouring one compound into another unless you know what you're doing. The nurses were doing just that … mixing all sorts of explosive elements.

I told her they were making a mistake. I could tell they were short-staffed, and if a problem broke out, the one deputy was the only one who could give them a hand. The nurse must have thought I was an alarmist. She merely smiled. "Officer, this isn't prison. It's a hospital."

"A hospital jail ward, ma'am," I said, more to remind than to correct her.

"Everyone's fine. All the patients are together watching TV and getting along. Don't worry, officer. Merry Christmas," she said, walking off.

Ten minutes later the same nurse came racing up the hall from the recreation room. "Hurry, we need your assistance. Some of the patients are fighting."

"Get the deputy. I can't leave here," I said.

"He's already there, but he can't stop them alone. You've got to come."

"Why did I ever accept the overtime?" I remember thinking. "Now what am I going to do?" Because of the power of the Correctional Officers Union, there weren't many rules that could result in termination if an officer broke them. But I knew a correctional officer leaving an escorted inmate unattended would bring instant termination. But I also knew that if I didn't go help the sheriff, the word would get out that a San Quentin guard wouldn't go help a fellow law enforcement officer. Not only would it go badly for me with the deputies from then on, but the officers at San Quentin would hear that I "pissed on myself," and they would start avoiding me.

I went up to the lone deputy in the control booth. Rattled, he had already called for reinforcements, but he told me they wouldn't arrive for half an hour. Meanwhile, the fight was getting worse. A dozen or more psychiatric patients and hospitalized inmates were breaking up the recreation room. He asked me to get down there and help his partner and the orderly.

"Look, you know the rules," I told the deputy. "I can't leave my prisoner."

"Normally I'd agree with you. But that old blind guy you're watching is blind and harmless. He's not going anywhere. You gotta get down to the rec room."

As I turned and started down toward the end of the hall, I could see people struggling on the floor. The nurses were getting the worst of it. I wasn't worried about the inmates as much as I was the psychos. I knew Mace wouldn't work on them. I didn't have a gun or a Rudy-club. It would have to be hand-to-hand. That's why the sheriff's department usually had two deputies working the ward. Christmas had lulled everybody into thinking there would be peace on earth ... and in the lockup hospital ward, too. Big mistake.

I reached the recreation room and found that a large male orderly had started ordering a group of patients back to their rooms. Right behind him, nurses were appearing, carrying syringes to sedate the wilder patients. Like driving wild cattle into pens, the orderly and I started shoving each struggling inmate into a room where we held him down while the nurse jabbed a needle into his butt. Once each patient started quieting down, we went back into the hallway, locked the door, and went after the remaining patients in the hall. We were winning the battle … but there was one big son of a bitch who was holed up in the corner of the recreation room, throwing food, books, lamps—anything he could get hands on—at the staff. I knew once we had him under control the fight would be over.

The orderly told me we were going to have to get the last patient into a room around the corner which contained a restraining bed. On a count of three, we rushed the inmate. It was like trying to pin down a Brahma bull. He was kicking, punching, biting, with the incredible strength of someone on PCP. But it was a worse chemical: pure adrenaline pumping through a madman's body.

The nurse was trying to hold his arms while the orderly squatted on his chest and I gripped both of his legs. One leg snapped loose and kicked a nurse in the stomach before she could jab the patient with the sedative. She rolled across the floor, and the orderly and I started dragging the patient toward the restraining room. He was fighting every inch of the way down the hall. I don't know how we did it, but we finally got him into the room that had a restraining bed bolted to the floor. Pushing him onto the bed, we started working him onto his back so we could get the restraining bolts down on his legs, chest, and arms.

All of a sudden, he started choking and drooling.

"He's having a seizure," cried the nurse.

The orderly loosed his grip from around his throat to let the man breathe.

"Hold on to him," I ordered. "I can tell he's faking."

Too late. With a jerk like someone getting an electrical jolt, the patient yanked an arm free, grabbed something from under the bed, and hit me in the knee. I toppled forward on the restraining bolt, which tore through my knee joint. I rolled onto the floor, blood spurting from my leg where he had stabbed me with a sharp pin from the restraining bolt I had fallen on.

Knocking the pin out of his hand, the orderly pushed the inmate back on the bed. Then the orderly and I threw ourselves across his body, holding him down long enough for a doctor to run in with sedatives and jab them through the patient's gown. At first, it didn't do any good. The patient was breaking loose again.

Bleeding from the knee and the mouth where he had punched me in the hall, I lifted up as high as I could and tried to immobilize him while they went to get another sedative. I was going to pass out from the pain, I thought, but I couldn't let go. None of us could. If the patient got on his feet, we were through. He would have been unstoppable.

We kept waiting for the sedative to take effect, but his struggling didn't subside. It seemed like the tranquillizers were making him stronger.

Glancing down, I saw my knee had swollen up like a melon. Using the pin he stabbed me with, I tore open my pants and couldn't believe what I saw: Aside from blood seeping out of my knee, it was completely black.

Minutes later, three deputies arrived to help. Within seconds, they had the wild man strapped down on the bed, and the next sedative did the trick, knocking him out cold. One of the nurses brought me a wheelchair to take me down to the emergency ward, but I told her I couldn't leave my prisoner unattended. I would be fired. She rolled me down to the nurse's station, where I called San Quentin.

Four times I had to telephone until certain the lieutenant got my message: I had been wounded in a fight at the jail ward and needed a replacement immediately. But no one showed up from the prison.

While I waited, nurses put temporary bandages around the stab wound in my leg and my shattered knee. No doctor was available to examine me. They were all down in the emergency room dealing with all the people who showed up on Christmas night, injured from drinking, fighting, and car accidents.

Around 10 p.m. a correctional officer I knew showed up.

"What the fuck took you so long?" I yelled.

Haines looked at my trousers, cut open to the knee, my bandaged knee, and my torn, blood-spattered uniform shirt. "Shit, the lieutenant didn't tell me it was an emergency. I stopped off and had dinner."

Haines quickly called San Quentin and got the Transportation Office on the line. "Hey, you guys, Woolf's really hurt." Soon as he hung up, Haines came out of the nurse's station. "The lieutenant's really sorry. He thought you just fell down or something. They're gonna send someone over her to get you and your car."

"Right, that fuckin' car's more important than me. You tell that son of a bitch lieutenant, when I see him, I'm going to take my good leg and stick it all the way up his ass."

Hines took my place guarding the blind man who had slept through everything that had happened. Then I was wheeled downstairs to be treated. I couldn't believe the state of the emergency ward. It was like a Civil War dressing station. Blood was splattered across the floor and down the wall. It was like somebody had come in with a machine gun and shot the hell out of twenty people.

The orderly wanted me to get up on a gurney with blood still smeared on it.

"You got to be kidding," I said. "Get someone to wash that first."

"Sorry. We're understaffed tonight."

"Don't I fuckin' know it, but clean that shit up or I'm not moving out of this wheelchair."

They got a janitor to scrub down the gurney and throw a clean sheet on it.

I couldn't lie down. It hurt too much. I sat up for three hours, waiting my turn for treatment—while heart attack victims were wheeled past on stretchers, a kid who swallowed a safety pin was treated, and a drunk who had fallen through a window was bandaged up. Finally, at one thirty in the morning, I was rolled into the treatment room.

The x-rays told the whole story. My knee looked like a snowball hit by a hammer.

"We can keep you overnight for observation if you wish, Officer Woolf," the doctor said.

"You kidding? Not in this place."

He had the nurse give me a shot for the pain and told me to go to my own hospital to have the knee treated. He said I would be unable to work circulation for several months.

I called Amy and told her what happened and to come get me. She thought it would be wiser if I went back to San Quentin for treatment.

"No fuckin' way!," I snapped, regretting the tone I used the second I had.

Amy came as fast as she could.

She helped me into the car and we started back to Marin County. Even though I was in a lot of pain, I knew I had to go back to work the next day—but I didn't think I could stand on my leg.

I told Amy I was worried about what would happen if I had to take time off because of my knee. I'd have to get a medical evaluation from a prison doctor. If I was ordered to take medical leave, my basic salary would be covered, but I would lose all my overtime should I be put on the extended injury list. I didn't want to risk it.

"Don't worry," she said. "We've lived on peanut butter and rice crackers before. We can do it again."

I think Amy was trying to make me feel better by exaggerating how bad it might get. But I was worried. I knew for a fact that if I couldn't pull in the ninety-six-hour shifts of work and overtime every week, my wages would plunge from $6,000 down to $875.

And Amy and I were way overextended with our rent, two cars, credit cards, and extra medical costs for her. I knew I had to keep working.

The next day I went to Kaiser Hospital to see my own doctor. After an examination and several x-rays, he said I needed an operation on my knee, and that I would need at least a month of bed rest. Was there any way, I asked, that I could put a brace on my knee and try to hide my limp until my knee got better?

"No way," he replied. "It'll only get worse."

I asked him to schedule the operation as soon as possible.

It would be nine weeks before they could schedule me for an operation. I called the administration office at San Quentin. I didn't want to let them know about the operation, so I just told them that I had been hurt and would need thirty days medical leave.

"Okay," the clerk said, making it sound real simple.

Within minutes, by the time I had finished answering all his questions, I was no longer a correctional officer on active duty, but one on medical leave. I didn't want to let them know about the operation.

Soon forms started arriving from the Department of Corrections. With each set of duplicate papers to fill out and sign, I could see I had fallen into a bureaucratic maze: I would have to apply for sick leave and disability and to use my vacation time. All the forms took time to go into effect. And in the interim, the only thing we had to live on was my monthly check.

I couldn't ask the bank for a loan. Technically, I wasn't working, and Amy and I had no mortgage to use as collateral. We were renting. And we owed too much on the cars to sell them.

We were forced to live on a strict budget. No more eating out. No more trips to Disneyland. The proverbial shit hitting the fan occurred exactly thirty days later.

We ran out of cash and credit, having just enough for rent and food, but beyond that we were broke.

I learned it would take 60 to 90 days to receive sick leave and that was only my basic salary, not enough to cover the bills we had accumulated. I couldn't go out and find a temporary job, and Amy was too fragile to work. Besides, she needed to stay home with the children. As for help from my family, I couldn't expect anything. My father was in prison and Griff was in a half-way house. Gina couldn't help me, and Kelly, Mandy, and Doris wouldn't. They said they had pressing financial problems of their own.

As for my drinking buddies from San Quentin, they were still meeting after work, but without me. It was as though I had moved away from the circle and it had closed up without my absence being noticed or making any difference.

Nine years working inside San Quentin, and all of a sudden I felt like the invisible man. Not one guard called to ask how I was. The only time someone telephoned from the prison was to ask me to clarify an answer I had given on one of the forms.

As the bills started to mount, the calls changed from polite reminders that a payment was past due to threats that the account would be turned over to a collection agency.

I decided the only thing left for me was to sue San Francisco General Hospital and the San Francisco Sheriff's Department for negligence in being understaffed on Christmas Day, which lead to my being seriously injured.

My attorney called back in three days with bad news. Although I was injured while on duty, I was not in Marin County when the injury occurred. I was in San Francisco.

"What difference does that make?" I snapped.

"San Francisco has a Fireman's Rule. A state employee cannot sue as the result of an injury incurred while assisting other state employees in an emergency."

Getting back to work was my only chance. Bankruptcy was too painful to imagine. Two months passed, and I had the operation. While still in the recovery room, I asked the surgeon to arrange physiotherapy sessions for me. Within two weeks, a physiotherapist was coming twice a week. I wasn't waiting around for him, though. I was trying to walk more and more every day—but my knee would keep buckling, and Amy or one of the children would have to help me up. I couldn't get up on my own.

After another month with little progress in walking, I made another appointment with my doctor to ask what kind of therapy I needed to walk again and how quickly I would regain full use of my knee.

He wasn't optimistic. "It's all a question of time."

"That's what I don't have."

He gave me a pep talk about how I should be grateful I hadn't been stabbed in the heart. But as well-meaning as his words were, they were worthless to me. I insisted on seeing a specialist.

After an extensive examination, the doctor, an expert in sports medicine, started off by echoing the diagnosis of my own physician, but then went on to make things worse. "A knee is one of the most problematic zones in the body," he said. "Once it's injured, it has its own laws of recovery that don't pertain to other areas, like the back, the shoulder, or the arm."

"So what can I do to speed up my recovery?"

"Nothing, or you'll actually delay it."

I decided to fake it—to pretend my knee was all better. Going home, I wrapped an Ace bandage around my knee and pretended to be walking up on the tier again, moving up and down the stairwells, imagining prison doctors were watching me and not inmates. I had to fool them that I was all better ... until I really was. I couldn't limp, couldn't grip my knee when it thudded with pain, but most of all, I couldn't buckle when all the strength dropped out of my knee. Three times I made it around the living room before everything gave out at once and I fell to the floor, looking up and imagining myself lying on the tier, except now it wasn't with the doctors saying, "No, you can't come back," but with the inmates leering at me saying, "We got you, motherfucker."

I was through at San Quentin. I knew it, but I couldn't admit it.

Later, I tried to look back at that day and see the difference—as though I had been walking on a mountain trail and had slipped, but the slope wasn't steep and I was merely down, ready to get back up, but when I couldn't, the slope seemed to get steeper and steeper, until the slope was gone, and it was a straight cliff I was grabbing onto, with Amy, Gail, and Brian holding onto me. When I couldn't hold on any more, I let go. And we all fell.

Sick leave was used up; vacation pay had been paid. No more financial buffers to count on.

The landlord let us fall behind a month with the rent, but when I couldn't come up with all of it for the second month, he gave us three days to pay the money, or he'd give us notice.

We sold one car to cover the rent. With the leftover money, we bought groceries. Our lifestyle seemed to vanish. We were used to living well. The children had clothes when they needed them. Amy could always have medicine that wasn't covered by Kaiser. Now everything but the most essential became a luxury. The children tried to understand what was happening—but they couldn't. It was embarrassing to them that they couldn't go to the movies with friends or have the money to go whale watching. They stayed at home more and more ... the four of us, like shipwrecked sailors, carefully meting out the provisions we had left. I couldn't believe my monthly check could vanish within days. The rent, insurance for the car, medical costs, food, telephone—all piranhas gobbling up the money, until there was nothing left. It was my fault. I had been spoiled, and in turn, spoiled everyone else in my family. The good times were over, and we would have to wait out the bad ones. Amy tried to get a job, but no one would hire her. She was too thin, too preoccupied, like someone always somewhere other than where she was. I spent time with the children, trying to make up for the time when I had been away. But the children sensed I wasn't home for them, but for myself. I had nowhere else to go. It was hard for me sitting around doing nothing. At San Quentin there was always the constant presence of inmates to keep me alert. I had never stopped moving. Now I felt myself edgy with nothing to do.

I waited for my knee to get better—but it didn't. I could never walk more than twenty minutes before pains would start shooting through my leg, and I could feel the knee starting to wobble. And if I could see the tremor beneath my trouser leg, so would doctors and staff—and so would inmates.

I would be a risk to the people I worked with and a target for those I guarded.

After six months, the administration must have decided to put me out of my misery. I was given early retirement under the California Industrial and Disability Act.

My monthly salary ended and my monthly disability payment began. The disparity staggered me: five hundred dollars less. Now I had to get a job. There was no more hope of getting back to San Quentin and working my way back up to earning, with massive overtime, the equivalent of more than three salaries a month. I would have to find something modest, something where I didn't have to run or walk too far. Within a week, I found a job as a dispatcher at a security company. I had done security work before and knew all the radio commands. The job didn't pay well, but it let me stay off my feet while I tried to look for another one.

After a couple of months, I borrowed enough money to start a small maintenance company—being owner and staff all rolled into one. Using crutches at first and then a cane, I would get off security patrol, then go clean offices I had been guarding hours before.

One night I got a phone call from a buddy at San Quentin. He said the lieutenant who had been on duty the night I was wounded had been taken off transportation duty because of incompetence. And now he had messed up again on a block and been fired.

The next day I telephoned my attorney to see if the officer's firing could help me win a case against the Department of Corrections. They had treated me so poorly, I was ready to sue them. He was sorry to inform me that my injury had taken place in San Francisco County, not in Marin County. And even though I had been working for a state agency, the responsibility wasn't theirs. "Besides," he added, "you stand to jeopardize your status by going after the very people giving you your monthly disability check."

"Just another two hundred and fifty dollars thrown away," I said when receiving the attorney's fee for taking time to answer my question. I quit thinking about suing. I just wanted to survive.

What made all the difference was that Amy and I were together. I wasn't drinking and she wasn't hiding from me. Within six months, though, we had lost the other car, had to move into a smaller apartment with the children, and finally, we had to do the one thing we didn't want to do: go bankrupt. But Amy realized it wasn't my fault we had to start from zero. More importantly, she saw how hard I was trying to find work outside of prison. We wouldn't give up.

Slowly the money I was making, along with my retirement check, began pushing the debts back. Things were turning around. My maintenance company got more clients, and I was able to hire three employees to take my place cleaning offices at night. Amy's health was improving, and she was even putting on weight. Brian and Gail were getting good grades in school. And a second operation had improved my knee to where I could stand for hours without having my leg buckle.

We had gone into a long tunnel, but we were coming out the other end.

"No matter what," I told her, "nothing will ever come between us again."

I didn't think to say … no one.

-#-

20

Overtime Burnout

One phone call blew up my life better than any bomb could have. It couldn't have gone off at a better time to maim Amy and destroy all of the trust she had been building up with me. It could have been a wrong number, but it wasn't. It was the wrong caller, though. "Hey, Rudy Boy, I've got a secret," said my father, his voice thick with cockiness.

"We've all got secrets," I replied.

"Yeah, but I got a big secret."

"So what's your big secret?"

"I just got a phone call from this gal in Louisiana named Diane."

Sixteen years vanished in an instant.

"Fuck!," I thought, believing I had taken care of her. Now my father knew.

Diane, the dancer from Pandora's Box. We had gotten involved right after we met. I started seeing her on the side when Amy and I were fighting about my not being home, which only got worse after I met Diane.

Then Amy left me and I gravitated toward Diane, seeing her more and more frequently. Stupidly, I took her to have dinner with my father one night at Joe's in San Rafael. I thought, "Well, here I am, with a woman classier and better looking than he ever had." I wanted to show my father that I could be like him—being married but still fucking a good-looking woman. I was as good as he was.

What a gathering that night. Griff came with his girlfriend, my father brought his latest, and I was with Diane. It was like the good old times in North Beach, with liquor and laughter flowing.

As though meeting my family was a sign I was serious about Diane, she started asking me when I was going to divorce my wife. From the beginning I had told her about Amy but said we had separated. I didn't try to stop Diane from thinking I was going to divorce Amy so I could marry her. But I wasn't serious. I just wanted to keep her happy while I was having fun.

A few months into my relationship with Diane, Amy and I started getting back together. We said it was for the children's sake—but I think we were too dependent on each other, for the right or wrong reasons, to continue being apart again.

All this time I was trying to get Diane to accept that it wasn't going to be a simple matter, divorcing Amy. I had to move slowly, so that the children weren't hurt. I was serious about the children, but I was hiding the truth from Diane. I didn't want to break up with Amy, yet I still wanted to have my on-going relationship with Diane. To keep from feeling guilty about Amy, I kept telling myself, "Well, the marriage could break up again for good. And then where would you be?"

I even managed to make up a story about transporting a prisoner to Los Angeles so that I could get away for a few days with Diane. The lie didn't bother me until I came back and walked in the house and found Amy sitting on the sofa with Gail and Brian. They all looked up, happy to see me.

"How was your weekend? Hope it wasn't too tiring," said Amy, as Gail ran over to hug me.

I couldn't look them in the eyes and went to take a shower.

That's when I realized I had to pull out of the relationship with Diane. But like those Chinese bamboo traps, it's much easier putting your finger in than getting it out.

Diane began putting more on more pressure on me—to spend the night with her instead of leaving at 1 a.m. There was another problem. Diane used more drugs than I ever had. I was trying to stay clean and keep my promise to Amy, but soon I was smoking a joint or doing a line with Diane.

The drive back to Marin got worse and worse. Crossing the Golden Gate Bridge in the fog, I felt like a bigamist who had only two half lives, not a whole one. Amy didn't make it easier. She never questioned me about where I had been. It made my secret dirtier. Diane, though, started questioning me about our own relationship. I knew that if I didn't act fast, I would lose her, so I bought her an engagement ring. For a while, I was able to stay in the downward spiral of being married to one woman while getting engaged to another. When Amy asked me what happened to the money in the bank account which I had spent on the engagement ring, I said I had lost it gambling. It was more truth than lie.

Finally, I had enough of trying to handle my secret life, so I decided to break with Diane. Taking a suit with me to San Quentin, I changed after work and drove to San Francisco. I took Diane to the Papagaya Room at the Fairmont Hotel, thinking that it would be easier to let her down in a nice place. I just couldn't get up the nerve. She must have sensed I was troubled about something, for she blurted out loud enough for other diners to hear, "So when are you gonna leave your wife?"

I leaned forward so only she could hear. "I'm not."

Diane turned as crimson as her hair. "Getting second thoughts, huh?"

"I've always had them. I'm tired of sneaking home and lying to my wife about where I've been. Let's cut our losses and end it."

I drove her home without accompanying her upstairs.

For the next few weeks, I dreaded that she would turn up at our front door to tell Amy what I had done. But she didn't call for a while. And when she did, it wasn't to ask if I had changed my mind about leaving. She wanted to inform me that she was pregnant.

We met in the city. I was panicked that Amy would find out and I would be through. I told Diane that I wanted to be part of the child's life … if she wanted to have it; if she wanted to have an abortion, then I would help her financially. The choice was hers.

Diane wasn't out for money. She really wanted the baby—and me now more than ever, if I would leave my wife.

I told her that, no matter what, I couldn't do it. "You have to decide what's best for you and the baby."

Months went by without a word from Diane. I didn't know what had happened to her, but I figured the best thing to do was to put the whole matter behind me.

When I first met her, I told her I was a law enforcement officer but didn't say where I worked. The only phone number she had to reach me was my cell phone. I thought I had done a good job of erasing any direct path to Amy and me. Bad luck would have it that Diane's sister knew a lady who had a friend whose husband was a correctional officer who knew me. It was a long, circuitous path—but it still lead to me.

One day working in the Reception Center, I got a phone call from Sergeant Kerner in the Reception Office. "Hey, Rudy, try to get someone to relieve you so you can go out and make a call. Your wife just called to say she gave birth to a baby boy."

I was stunned. Some of the other officers saw how pale I was after the call and thought someone had died. In a way, someone had: me. I got permission to go make a phone call and telephoned Diane at her apartment. Her sister answered. Sure enough, Diane had given birth to a son and was at San Francisco General. I went back to the Reception Center and talked to Sergeant Kerner. There were a couple of other officers present when I said that it wasn't my wife who called about giving birth to my son. I filled him in on who she was. The other officers started laughing. They were all married, and I could see them trying to imagine themselves in such a situation. After the laughter died out, their expressions of sympathy began. "You're fucked, Woolf."

I got another officer to take my shift, and I called my house. When Amy answered, I told her I had a chance for an easy job on overtime. I raced to San Francisco still in my uniform, parked the car from the hospital, and started for the entrance. With each step, my legs got heavier. All the worst scenarios started appearing. Either way, I was finished. For a moment, I thought of going to borrow money from friends and taking off to some place like Bulgaria to start life all over again under a different name. But I couldn't abandon Amy, let alone Gail and Brian.

I got in the hospital elevator and started up to the maternity floor. I was ready to face Diane, but then, thud, the elevator stopped and the door opened between floors. I found myself staring at a stone wall. That's all it took. I don't believe in symbols, but if I ever wanted to see one, there it was.

Returning to the lobby, I found a pay phone and called Diane's room. A nurse answered. "Just tell her that I'm sorry," I said. "I'm a coward. I can't come see the baby. Tell her to forgive me."

The nurse must have known what was going on for she didn't say a word; she just hung up. I knew what I had said was cold.

As the weeks passed and I didn't hear from Diane, I began to worry about her. I went by Pandora's Box to see if she had returned to work. From what I gathered from one of the dancers, Diane had been laid off.

It seemed like a cruel way for the dancer to put it. But she didn't mean anything. I was the one who was cruel. I drove to Diane's apartment and learned she had moved out. The decision to continue looking for her made me feel like I was entering a cave whose size I had no idea of. It was dark; that's all I knew. But I had to find out what had happened to Diane and the baby.

After contacting a cop buddy who worked the Tenderloin district, I learned that Diane was living in a rundown apartment building on Eddy near Taylor.

The front door was wide open. I glanced at the names on the mailbox and then went upstairs and knocked on the door.

"Who is it?" she asked.

"Me."

The door opened. It was Diane, but a different one than I had known. She looked drawn and haggard, her sweater stained. The living room was a mess.

"How'd you find me?"

"Did I ask you that when you called me at San Quentin?"

She tried for a smile and let me in. We had a drink and talked. I kept looking around. She must have guessed for what. "He's sleeping in the bedroom," she said.

Now that I was there, I didn't know what I was going to do.

If my father had been there, he might have thrown a wad of cash on the table and said, "Here. Deal with it. Don't ever contact me again or I'll beat the shit out of you. Just keep that fuckin' kid and yourself away from me." Or the flip-side would have been, "Hey, if it was that good, let's fuck again. Except this time, if you get pregnant, we're gonna use a coat hanger."

"What do you want to do?" she finally said.

"See him."

"You sure?"

"Yeah. Otherwise I wouldn't have come."

She must have struggled with the decision. Several minutes passed. All the time she was sitting there, staring at me, not saying a word. Just when I was going to get up and leave, she walked into the other room and moments later came back holding a blue-eyed baby wrapped in a blanket. "Here's your son," she said, handing him to me.

I took him in my arms and stared down at the face ... which stared back at me with the impossible gaze all babies have as if they know everything there is to know about you, yet they don't look away. I was ready to crack. I felt my eyes glass over. I had to get out of there, and I knew when I did, I wouldn't just be saying I was a coward over the phone; I'd be one in real life. After another moment, I handed her back the baby and got up. "Here," I said, putting an envelope on the table.

"What's that?"

"Three thousand dollars. It's all I can afford."

"I don't want your money."

"Take it. You need it. I know you're not dancing any more."

She started to push the envelope back.

"No, take it. I'm not trying to buy you."

Diane looked up as though she were staring up from the bottom of a well. "Can't you just be with us?"

To answer, I couldn't look her in the eyes. "No, I can't leave Amy. Please understand."

"Why not?"

"Don't ask me, Diane. I can't abandon my kids.... like my father did with us. My children aren't throwaways."

"So you'll throw away your own child with me."

I couldn't answer. She was right. "I'd better go," I finally muttered, starting to leave.

"Rudy, can you do me a favor?"

"Anything ... well, almost anything. What?"

"I need to get to Concord. Will you take us?"

Minutes later, I was driving over the Bay Bridge with Diane and the baby. I kept glancing over, imagining Amy driving by with one of her girlfriends who would spot me and say, "Oh, look, Amy, there's Rudy. Who's the woman with the baby?" But I got safely to Concord. The stores were open late, and I could see that Diane needed clothes. And babies always needed more diapers. So I pulled into a shopping center, and for the next hour we went through one department store after another, going up one aisle after another, buying clothes for the baby and Diane. She kept asking if I wanted to know the baby's name. I knew she had been holding it back as a surprise. But I told her it was not a good idea to tell me. It would make it harder to leave him when I did.

An hour later we arrived back in front of her apartment in San Francisco. Hurriedly, I got the shopping bags from the back and carried them upstairs while Diane got out with the baby. I didn't want to stick around. I was ready to go and Diane could see me doing everything I could to get out of there—and back to where Amy, Gail, and Brian were waiting for me.

"Rudy, I wasn't going to tell you and leave you feeling guilty about what would happen to us. But I met someone real nice in Golden Gate Park. Frank's divorced and from Louisiana. He just got out of the Army and he wants me to marry him and take me back to Alexandria with him. He says he wants my son to grow up as his own son. Now that you've told me your decision, I'm going to make mine. I'm going with him."

I was relieved, but I didn't want to show Diane. She might think it was from knowing that I was off the hook. That was part of it, but the relief also came from knowing that she wouldn't be living in the Tenderloin.

Clutching the baby, she kissed me goodbye.

That was the last time I ever saw Diane.

When the second shoe finally fell, it was filled with lead.

After a silence of three years during which I had quietly buried all memories of Diane and the incident, I got an official letter from the California Bureau of Child Support. Because I had been listed as the birth father of a child on welfare in New Orleans, the State of Louisiana petitioned their counterpart agency in California to collect child support on behalf of my son.

I went to see an attorney in San Francisco. She wanted to fight the paternity charge, but I didn't want to create any more trouble than I had. Louisiana wanted six hundred dollars a month; we finally agreed on two.

Now I had to take on more overtime to cover up the two hundred a month, and twenty-four hundred dollars a year was no small piece of change.

My dreams started getting pretty raw. In fact, I think they were mostly nightmares. I started seeing a therapist on the side. What the hell, another couple of hundred a month was worth it if I could talk to someone about what was going on in my life. I sure couldn't tell my father or brother or any of my sisters. As for the guys at work, they were too busy having affairs of their own to want to hear about what had happened because of mine.

The two hundred was hush money. I lived with it. It was a consequence of fucking up. Once I quit thinking about the amount being taken the first of every month from a separate account I created so that Amy wouldn't find out, I forgot about it.

Thirteen years later I was home with Amy, Gail, and Brian when the phone rang.

Amy answered it. "Yes it is. Yes he is. Who should I say it is?" She handed the phone to me. "It's some woman named Diane calling from Louisiana."

I must have shown the shock I felt, for Amy looked at me with concern. "You okay?"

"Yeah, just getting a migraine." I look the phone and tried to keep my hand from shaking.

"Hello?"

"Say hello to your son, Rudy Boy."

I glanced over at Amy sitting next to me. Breaking off talking with the children, she sensed something was up and she was studying me, trying to figure out what was going on.

"Hello, this is Charles," said a young man, his voice still high and unbroken.

"Hello, Charles. How you doing?"

As he started talking, I tried to make my responses sound appropriate to him and to Amy both.

"I always wanted to talk to you," Charles said softly.

"Yeah, I always wanted to say hello to you, too," I replied. "How are your folks?"

"Fine."

I couldn't allow myself to start thinking or I was lost. I had to do what I did in prison a thousand times when faced with a threat: bluff my way through. And I did.

We talked for another ten minutes, and then I asked Charles to let me speak with his mother.

"Really a nice surprise hearing from you," I said, trying to sound pleased.

"I didn't want to bother you, but Charles started asking all sorts of questions about his father I couldn't answer."

"Well, listen, I'd love to talk about this more, but I'm sort of busy. Give me a call tomorrow sometime and we can take care of everything."

I hung up.

Amy was right in my face. "Why are you talking to some woman's kid? Who's she?"

When you're crossing an abyss on a tightrope, you don't stop to admire the view. You keep moving. So I muddled through, telling her that Diane was the wife of a correctional officer I had known. Now he was getting close to retirement and wanted to get advice about his life insurance policy.

"What does life insurance have to do with you?"

"I used to sell it, remember? I was good, too."

Within a few minutes, I had Amy feeling guilty for putting me through an inquisition.

About two minutes from having a major stroke, I had to go for a walk.

I realized Diane had my home phone number, but how did she get it when I was unlisted? I figured out what to do to make certain that Diane couldn't ever reach me at home. When I got to work, I called Amy to say that I had been contacted by the security unit. I told her that an inmate had gotten a look at staff phone numbers, and that mine was among them. I called Pacific Bell to ask for another unlisted number. Amy was glad. She didn't want anything to do with prison coming into our home. Of course, I told my father, Griff, and my sisters the new number, but no one else.

Two days later while Amy was preparing dinner and the phone rang, I wasn't nervous. It wouldn't be Diane. No, it could only be someone who knew my new number.

It was my father with his big secret. If ever I've heard the voice of someone who was sitting on a gold mine, it was his. He couldn't wait to tell me a few days before Diane reached me at home that she had called information to find a Rudy J. Woolf in Marin County.

Being a correctional officer, my phone number was unlisted.

Sure enough, though, Diane was given Rudy J. Woolf's number, except it wasn't my number: It was my father's. Of all the people in the world Diane could have called, she telephoned the one person who would lead her to me, his own namesake: my father. And when she called, it just happened to be on one of the rare nights when he was home. When he answered, she asked to speak with Rudy J. Woolf.

"This is Rudy Woolf," he said.

She must have thought it was me after all the years, so she started talking to him about his son.

"What the fuck are you talking about?" he said. "I don't have any kids with you."

"Yes, you know you do, a sixteen-year-old son."

My father said the conversation got pretty weird about then. "Look, I got two sons from one woman," he told her, "and I have a couple of more floating around somewhere, but I know their mothers don't want them to have anything to do with me."

"Then I guess he's kinda like you."

"What are you talking about?"

"He never wanted to be my son's father." About then, she must have realized that she wasn't talking to me, so before hanging up, she asked my father if he knew another Rudy J. Woolf.

"Just my son."

"Did he ever work at San Quentin?"

Bing! The sixty-four thousand dollar question. Then it was my father's turn to start asking questions. He told me it was the longest phone conversation he ever had.

And now he was bragging about everything he had learned. I knew it was too much to think that he would let it go at that. I was right. He had a little favor to ask. Having lost his license to sell automobiles because of his felony convictions for identity fraud, he needed me to take one out in my name so he could use it to make money.

I refused. I knew that within hours of getting the license he would be wheeling and dealing. Scams would occur. The police would be called in, and they would trace everything back to the Rudy J. Woolf who signed the license application.

Instead of working at a prison I would be doing time at one. And if there is one thing a correctional officer knows, it's that he never wants to be put away, because every inmate in the country is going to know that a former guard has just arrived … as a prisoner. And he can start counting the days he has left to live on one finger.

So, I told my father no, again.

But he never liked no. He never learned what it meant. So he kept raising his voice. His request finally removed the fancy lining and revealed itself for what it was: a threat. "Rudy, Rudy, that'd be really bad if Amy found out about your little kid."

"Yeah, it would be. One of us would be dead."

"You threatening me, motherfucker?"

"Yeah."

"I'm not afraid to come over there and tell your wife that you knocked up some little bitch and she has a kid with you."

"Look, why do you have to be like this?"

For the first time in the conversation, he was silent. I could almost hear him thinking. He knew he had something big over me … what was the best way for him to use it?

Then I heard giggling in the background.

"Hey, who's with you?"

"Your sisters," my father said.

"Oh, you've already told them about what happened."

"Hey, I'm his grandpa. He's my business, too."

"You're nothing to him because I'm nothing to him."

"Oh, bullshit. I remember this little cunt. You took her to Joe's when you were fuckin' and going all over the place."

"It's really none of your business."

"It is my business, 'cause that's part of my sperm that's in that kid."

"What, did you fuck her, too?"

He started yelling and screaming, threatening to call the courts to make me pay child support.

"Too late. I've already been paying child support for thirteen years."

"What! You've kept this a secret for thirteen years?"

"Sixteen, if you wanna get it right.'"

"How come you didn't tell me?" he yelled.

"I would rather tell a stranger on the street than you. At least there would be more chance of getting some respect."

"Yeah, well, you wait till Amy finds out."

I was scared. Now it wasn't just my father who knew. It was Kelly and Mandy. With their non-stop mouths, soon all of Marin County would know.

All of a sudden, my father started humming, like some twelve-year old kid at the fun house. He was having a ball.

"Listen, you keep the fuck away from me and Amy," I shouted, and then hung up.

"What's wrong?" Amy asked, coming out of the kitchen.

"My father. He's been drinking."

"Oh," she said, going back to finish cooking dinner.

True to character, my father didn't listen to me. He called five times over the next two days, each time threatening to tell Amy if I didn't sign the sales license.

I refused each time he asked. Finally, it must have gotten through to him: I wasn't going to do what he said. Now it was his turn to hang up.

The next day my sister Doris called to say she heard there was another Woolf in the family.

"Don't listen to dad."

"It was Kelly who told me."

"Don't listen to her either."

"I can't believe it, keeping it a secret all this time."

"Well, I did."

"Why?"

"So you wouldn't find out."

"That's so mean," whined Doris. "Why don't you want us to know?"

"Because you're all hazardous to my health."

That weekend my father called back. "Look, I can't wait any longer. Either you sign the papers or I'm coming over to tell Amy tonight."

"Fuck you. Stay away."

"I'm coming over."

"If you do, I'm gonna have a shotgun waiting, and I'll blow your ass off the porch."

"You motherfucker, I'll have you killed for talking to me like that. Fuck that license. I'm telling her. Then I'm gonna kick your ass in front of your kids."

"Come on then, and take your best shot. 'Cause you only got one, old man."

That night after Amy and the kids went to sleep, I sat in the darkened living room. Sweating as I hadn't been since running in from the Adjustment Center yard, I waited for my father's footsteps on the porch the way I had listened for them as a boy. I knew when he came it would be bad. I had seen him in a bar fight with Griff only months earlier. When the bartender called the police to tell them who was fighting, they didn't just send two officers. They sent four and a

K9 dog. Still, it took all of them to subdue my father and Griff, who forgot their differences to take on the cops.

No, I knew he wouldn't back down. He probably took my threat seriously and had his .45 with him. Well, I had lied. There was no shotgun, but there was my service .38 and it was resting on my lap under a towel, so the children wouldn't see it if they got up to go to the bathroom in the night. "Patricide": I knew what the word meant. I looked it up once in the dictionary when I came across it in an article about domestic homicide. Now I was waiting to see if my father was going to kill me, or I him.

As he had already been to San Quentin, he'd go back for sure. As for me, if an ambitious prosecutor wanted to show premeditation, he could probably get one of my sisters to say I had threatened to kill my father. I'd end up on death row … maybe even go into that diving bell, and hear the door clank shut again, but it wouldn't be a test the next time.

But my father never showed up.

Amy was up first in the morning. When she nudged me awake, she didn't see the gun.

"What are you doing out on the sofa?"

"I couldn't sleep," I said, getting up and keeping the pistol concealed.

"What's the towel for?"

"I had a fever last night. I was sweating."

"You better take care of yourself."

I went back into the bedroom, put the pistol lock on the trigger, then slid it back under my socks inside the dresser. Walking back into the living room, I heard a car approaching the house. I glanced outside to make sure it wasn't a red Mustang.

I couldn't wait anymore. I didn't know if he was serious or not, but I couldn't take a chance. I couldn't let him tell her before I did. "Listen, Amy, I gotta talk to you."

"Not now. I have to make breakfast."

"It can't wait."

"Why not?"

"You'll know when I tell you."

-#-

21

Bottoming Out

Whoever said, "If you hit bottom falling in a dream you die," never did. You can hit bottom again and again and never die. Of course, you wish you had. After Amy divorced me because of Diane, I shut down. I don't even remember what happened for the next year ... except that everything that mattered seemed to have come to an end.

As I had done before at San Quentin, I buried myself in work. Not only was I given more hours at the security company, but when my knee got better from physical therapy, I got a promotion to supervisor. I was also running the maintenance company. Working both jobs meant not getting much sleep, but it didn't matter. I felt like a zombie no matter how many hours I slept. Amy didn't want to see me. I sent money for her and the children, but she never wrote or called. The only acknowledgement I would get that she had received the money was when the cancelled checks arrived from the bank.

She was through with me, I realized. All of the lies, all of the drinking, the drugs, the staying-out late, and the deceptions, small and large, had finally culminated with my confessions about Diane and the baby. There was one thing Amy had never done in all the years we had been together: stopped loving me. And now she had.

Life felt as hopeless as it had when I was eleven on the morning I learned my mother died.

I'm "doomed," I thought, just as I had been—even though I didn't know then the meaning of the word I now understood.

Alcohol seemed inadequate to help me forget all that I wanted to blot from my mind.

Drugs, too, were only a temporary means of distraction.

Like a dervish in the desert, I wanted to spin faster and faster until everything became a blur and I couldn't recognize anything—most of all myself. I succeeded.

It amazed me—how lost a person can get if no one else wants to find him.

-#-

22

Life Insurance

It was in the closet of the room I was renting in San Rafael, buried in a cardboard box under photo albums I had brought with me when Amy and I divided up our possessions. I hadn't played the tape in years. I wasn't even sure it would still work. But I put it in the small tape recorder I used for my security job—and pushed the play button.

Instead of standing in front of those hundreds of sales executives in San Francisco that night almost twenty-five years before, Norman Levine now had the perfect captive audience: a man lying on his back in a darkened room amid the wreckage of his life, with nothing to do but listen. They were the same words I had heard before but they weren't the same. Maybe I'm crazy, I thought, but the message didn't sound the same. It was as though large passages had been added to fill in the silence of the pauses … not to make the lecture longer, but to make the words sink in deeper. Adjusting the volume, I stretched back out, trying to imagine I was in that auditorium again, listening to Norman Levine say, "Believing is everything."

"The difference between unsuccessful people and successful people is that successful people will do what unsuccessful people won't. Not can't, won't. You've gotta do a lot of unpleasant things if you want to reach for a star you have not found yet. If you think you can do it the cheap way, you're taking a dive. My business is life. I'm in this business for life. Listen carefully. I'm in this business … for life. And you should be too. If you're not doing all you can to live your life, it doesn't count, it won't count. I'm sure that if you're listening to me, you're not satisfied with the way things are. For some of you, this feeling of frustration comes from not having achieved your level of competence and success. Regardless of your problem, there is a relatively simple solution to it. If there's one thing we know, it's that we're not immortal. If we don't use the life we've been given, shame on us. To live, we have to make a commitment to life. The only thing I ask you is, if you are going to fail, to fail with dignity. Don't try to drag everybody else down with you for what you have done. Don't blame your manager, the company, the product, your family, or your past. If you want to blame somebody, don't try to look at the person next to you. Look in the mirror. Following the sixty-percent attrition rate for our business, more than half of you will fail. But you don't have to. The moment you start talking negatively, you are going down, like a boxer getting in the ring and telling himself, 'I can't beat my opponent.' He is really defeating himself. I hear people screaming, 'Stop the world. I want to get off. Life hurts too much.' I know of only one way to get off this planet permanently, and given the choice I'd like to delay that as long as possible. One life, one world. Now I'm either going to adapt to this world, or I'm going to waste this one life."

I hit the stop button, hit reverse, then picked up the .38 pistol I had removed from the box before finding the tape. I put it back in the holster. I didn't need the gun anymore. If I had pulled the trigger, the wrong Rudy Woolf would have won, and the right Rudy Woolf would have lost.

I got up from the closet and looked around. What a mess. Gotta lot to do, I thought. Gotta turn the lights on first.

-#-

23

Struggling Up

More than inspired by the words on the tape, I felt cleansed of all that had happened, almost reborn. I renewed the life insurance license I had let expire and went back into sales. Within a week I started my own security company with fifty bucks and an auctioned police car with two hundred thousand miles on the engine. No matter. I painted the company logo on the doors and I was in business. The first few months I was the company receptionist and staff, taking phone calls during the day and then going out to patrol sites at night.

That summer, Amy forwarded a letter addressed to me without the name of the sender or a return address. As though to have the last word on my refusal to sign the sales license, my father, who had gone with Kelly to visit Mandy in Dallas, decided they should all go visit "the new Woolf member." Inside the envelope was a photograph of my father and my sisters posing with an older Diane and a tall boy with blonde hair.

My father was beaming as though he knew I would be looking at the photograph. I stared at the boy. He had the eager expression of someone who has won a prize at sports—just glowing with pride. I guessed it came from meeting the grandfather he had never known—and thinking maybe he'd get to meet his father, too.

As angry as I was at my father's revenge—Got you now, Rudy Boy"—I was more sorry for the boy, for I couldn't cross the distance between us. He and I would stay apart: the boy in the photograph and I, his father, looking at him.

I had to focus on the family I had in the place where I was. If I crossed the boundaries of my life with Amy, Gail, and Brian to get to know my lost son, I would be lost, too. I could never give him what he craved. I could only create more sadness for everyone—except for my father, who would have stood by watching everything fall apart and laughing the Woolf-laugh. No chance. I couldn't risk it. I had to focus on the here and now.

My company was expanding. With more and more violence in the cities, more and more people wanted private security for their homes or businesses. Within two years, I had twelve guards, two dispatchers, and one assistant working in a suite of offices in San Rafael.

Of course, my father heard about my success and got jealous. One day he called up looking for "Rudy Boy." My assistant corrected him by saying, "Don't you mean Mr. Woolf?"

"I'm Mr. Woolf, you bitch," he said, slamming down the phone.

A day later he called her back to say he had just bought the company from me and was coming over to "fire your ass and everyone else's."

Even though he was past sixty, my father looked twenty years younger: his hair still full, his physique still muscular, the smile still magnetic. The words were still honey coated when not razor-edged. His hocus pocus still potent, he had found a new arena for his charms. He was wooing widows out of money, saying he was a Hollywood producer putting together a picture deal and needing an advance until the studio's money kicked in. His attorney would be coming back from the Bahamas any day to fill them in on the details.

It always worked. For those ladies, being with my father was like being fanned by a tropical breeze. It felt so good they didn't think of anything else. When he had something to brag about, he'd call, insisting we have lunch. Then I would get to hear of his latest conquests. "I'll fuck more girls before I die than you've fucked all your life."

"Girls? You mean blue-haired ladies?"

"Better than that scrawny thing you're screwing."

"At least I'm Viagra-free."

So it went, playing our Dirty Dozen, neither of us capable of saying anything tender. A pathetic pissing-contest that had gone on too, too long.

Then came the car accident—the first. Doris was in a wreck on Arnold Drive. Both legs were amputated and doctors said she would be in a wheel chair for life. When we went to visit her, she displayed the true Woolf toughness, telling us, "If anyone calls me a gimp, I'm gonna kick their fuckin' ass."

That was the last time I saw my father for quite a while.

I put all my effort into my security company and taking care of things at home. Besides, I knew my father would do more than just get by on his own.

One morning, two years after divorcing me for the big lie, Amy telephoned to say she was willing to take me back.

"Why after all this time?" I asked.

"You originally got a life-sentence but I reduced it to two years because of good behavior."

She had seen I was clean every time I came to visit her, Gail, and Brian.

Drugs and booze were places in the past I didn't want to revisit. And I didn't want to bring them into the present.

And not working sixteen hours a day at San Quentin, I no longer needed the high adrenaline-fix. I realized I had gotten out before burning out as only a correctional officer can, leaving nothing but the shell of a man watching the end of his life rush toward him.

No, I was lucky. I still had a lot of time in front of me.

But at an age when most men have reached the pinnacle of their chosen careers, I had to start from scratch with another one.

I had to work hard to get the life I wanted—not the one we had, but one with both of us home at night with our children.

From time to time, I'd still run into old buddies from San Quentin. They'd ask if I was coming back. They knew I had retired, but they kept asking. I guess it was habit, or just their way of seeing how I felt about getting out. I was glad not to be walking the tiers.

Prisons were becoming more violent than ever. After I left, San Quentin's security level was changed. No longer a Level IV, maximum security, it was now Level II, along with becoming the Reception Center for felons moving from society into other prisons throughout the state. Now Pelican Bay was the max of maxes, a prison so modern that it was deemed barbaric in the eyes of the ACLU. Inmates were isolated twenty-three hours an day, causing many to succumb to depression and schizophrenia. But with the prison population growing all the time, and three-strike laws sending many more prisoners behind bars, prisons were providing the learning experience that families and schools once did.

And I knew that hundreds of thousands of violent young men would become more violent behind bars. Progressive thinkers were spouting off about modern prisons offering rehabilitation. Millions of dollars were spent on classes for educating inmates to improve themselves—but I knew it was gold dust tossed in the wind.

The lore of the gang was greater than any words of truth an inmate could read in a book. I knew the brutal truth. I remembered two brothers being in the same gang. To test one, the gang ordered him to kill his sibling. Depending on whether one values loyalty above human life, he passed. It was one of the most horrible memories I carried away from San Quentin. The way gangs were growing was like a horror movie when a monster is being pinned down with chains and tranquilizers. After a while, the drugs wear off and the monster breaks the chains and gets loose to terrorize everything in his path. That monster was the collective rage of the prison nation. And I knew it was coming our way because I helped chain the monster down for as long as I could.

Whenever I saw news about a guard being stabbed at a prison, I'd tell myself, "Rudy, that could have been you." Even though my knee still ached, I felt like a soldier with a hundred-dollar wound that got him out of the war and safely home. Home wasn't much, but light came through the windows, and I could walk outside by opening just one door.

Now that my son was a teenager, it wasn't long before my father started making overtures to Brian. I told him, "Your grandfather's a very powerful man. He always likes to have his way. He may try to get you to do things that you don't want to do. Just say "no." If he keeps pressuring you, call me."

After all these years, I had finally learned how to say no to him, but now I had to teach my son quicker than the lifetime it had taken me. Maybe as a way of making up for the time he didn't spend with me, my father devoted himself to Brian. He liked to take him to the movies. Of course, they were usually about criminals in the good old days. One night he took Brian to see a movie about Bugsy Siegel in Las Vegas. In the middle of the movie, my father started yelling loud enough for everyone in the theater to hear. "That's not the way he got killed, and he's not buried out in the desert, either. He's in the foundation of the Sands."

Needless to say, he made an impression on Brian—and the audience.

Then, six years later, I got a phone call in the middle of the night. On Arnold Road, the same one Doris had been driving down when she had her accident, Gina had been killed when a falling eucalyptus branch went through the car windshield and impaled her to the seat. Just as with the news of my mother's death, I had to go tell Griff that Gina was gone. After my mother, no one was closer to Griff than Gina. Now she, too, was gone.

My brother became even more than what he was since the age of eight—a special kind of orphan. Within weeks, Griff returned to the only place that would provide the kind of solace he needed: drugs. And, of course, with drugs went another arrest and another return to prison. It was as though Griff kept trying to find smaller and smaller islands inside himself where he could hide, except they weren't islands. They were cells surrounding him. I did all I could to be the big brother, keeping an eye out for him. But it was difficult helping him. For me, he resembled a little boat endlessly taking on water that had to be bailed out so it wouldn't sink. I wearied of the task. Besides, I had my own life to rescue. Amy, Gail, and Brian were counting on me; and for once I wouldn't let them down.

-#-

24

Wish Upon a Star

Time's strange. When I was working behind the walls, the seconds would drag on. Today, as president of my own security company, I find months evaporate like steam off coffee. Five years have passed since Amy and I renewed our marriage vows. We've been divorced, separated, and remarried so often we're not sure which day is our true anniversary: our original marriage or our second one. We decided to celebrate both. What matters is that we're still together. No more wall of lies between us. We work hard at maintaining our openness to each other.

For thirty-one years Amy has stuck by me—even if we weren't together for five of those. I guess I have finally become the man she had first glimpsed at a 7-Eleven store so long ago. The store's still there, but now it's my son who uses it—going back and forth from his job in sales, working for a benevolent despot, his old man. I know it's hard for Brian to take orders from the same person who jokes with him at night over the dinner table. But we'll work it out. Brian put an end to generations of Woolfs going to prison—one way or another. Only once did he ask me about following in my footsteps and becoming a correctional officer.

"Never. I'll go back there first," I said.

He must have understood how serious I was. He never brought the subject up again.

As for Gail, she is doing well. She lives in Hawaii, where she owns her own business on the island of Lanai. The four of us get together a few times a year, either or the holidays or on the children's birthdays.

Every once in a while, I tell myself, "Hey, you've only got a GED. You can't be the president of a company." But then another voice cuts in, "Come on, after all your time at San Quentin, you have a Ph.D. in abnormal psychology." Still, hiring people with skills and experience I don't have has made all the difference in achieving success. My security firm not only protects our clients from drug dealers, prostitutes, and street gang activity in low-income areas through Northern California, but we also assist in creating neighborhood-watch programs in upper-scale neighborhoods. In addition, we are developing plans with the state of California to help released sexual offenders get relocated in communities that don't want them. As a parent, I understand the fear of having a predator living down the block. But today, with chemical castration, monitoring devices—one to make certain a parolee stays within fifty feet of his address, and the other a global positioning system to track him wherever he goes—I think the danger is minimal. Besides, the man has paid his time. He deserves another chance. I got many more than I deserved.

Every once in a while, though, things will slow down at work, and I'll find myself thinking about the past. Sometimes I'll imagine myself walking up a hillside to look down at all my siblings to see how they are doing. Not a pretty sight.

Gina's dead. Doris is crippled physically. Griff's crippled mentally. Kelly's a bag girl for dad. Mandy's a "shopaholic" As for the older brother, the jury's still out on him. In my car I keep a little black box with no openings. But if I push a button on the bottom, a voice rises up: "Let me out. Will someone please let me out?"

A reminder of the past.

This afternoon I pick up my father for lunch. We see each other every few weeks. At sixty-seven, he is starting to have serious health problems. But an aging tiger is still a tiger.

Sitting across from him at the restaurant, I watch his gesticulating hands slice the air, reinforcing what he is saying more eloquently than the gestures of any rapper in the hood. Every female customer who passes, he has to ogle. As for the hostess, she gets the royal treatment: a bouquet of compliments. But I know the flowers are artificial, kept for just such occasions. I know; I used to hand them out myself. As he leans over to talk with two women at the next table, I smile. It's like it's always been. We're supposed to be having lunch together—but it's only him alone. I'm only here when he wants to tell me a story from the past—one I could repeat back to him word for word—or when he wants to tell me "to get fucked" for not spending more time with him.

Looking past the rose-colored lens of his thick glasses, I see the burning eyes that have stared at me since childhood. They haven't changed. The flames still flicker. I know that if a waiter spilled something on my father right now, he would be on his feet in an instant, doing whatever it took to restore his image of cool and studied elegance. He hasn't changed, and long ago I gave up wanting him to.

He is my father, an impossible country I will never be able to go far enough inside to know, so I remain at the border between his world and the world—knowing this spot is the only place to be with him ... forever.

As he gets up to leave, he grimaces at a pain in his leg. I reach over to help him up, but he pulls back. Still proud, still in charge of things. I never want to see him grow old. I want him to die in the middle of a story, the one he loves to tell me, where he was fucking a woman, and I knocked on the door. "Dad, dad," I cried. "You'd better stop, her husband just pulled into the driveway." They jumped up and dressed. My father ran to the window and peeked through the curtains. "What the fuck are you talking about?" he yelled. "He's not out there."

Beyond the door, I laughed, as I do again now, hearing my words coming from my father's mouth: "No, you little asshole, he's pulling into his driveway down the street." We laugh together.

Stopping in front of his house in San Rafael, I go around to open his door. He waves me off. "What the fuck do you think I am, a broad? And when you see your drug addict of a brother, tell the punk to get his ass up here to help me."

"Yes, Dad."

Moments later, he is walking up the steps. For a second, from the back, with his curly dark hair and wiry build, he looks the way he did coming home, when Gina, Griff, and I would look out the window ... to see by his movement if he were drunk or sober.

Now there is nobody home, nobody waiting for him. No one cares what he does.

I feel sorry for him. So many women and not one stayed around after the music stopped and the shouting began. I drive away, watching him in the rear-view mirror, to make sure he gets safely in. After all, he's still my father.

Commuter traffic is heavy, and it takes me an hour and a half to reach the cemetery in Colma. The guardian's starting to close the gates when I pull up, but a twenty dollar Rudy grants me a brief visit. I hurry down the alley until I find the grave I am looking for.

It looks the same as the day she was buried, I tell myself. But why wouldn't it? I sit down on the damp ground and put my hand on the tombstone. If only she could hear me ... but she can't. How would all of us be different if she hadn't fallen from that horse? Would Gina be alive? Would Doris be walking? Would Griff never have used drugs? And my father, how would he be different? Would mom have soothed and calmed the rage with time? Would he have finally put down the life of petty crime and become what he could have become: a great salesman? Last, where would I be if my mom hadn't been buried here since I was eleven? Everything would have been different for all of us.

I know there will be no answer to my questions. But that's what graves are for, I suspect: for the dead to listen to the living.

Coming back up Highway 101 through Marin, I take the Larkspur exit and follow the winding road to the berths at Paradise Cove. I don't like coming here, but I promised Griff I'd check in on his boat. He can't bring himself to come out and clean it. I don't know what it is about his boat that makes him jumpy. He lived on it for months, and he kept telling me he was going to sail off to the South Seas and find a job as a bartender and lie around on the beach, watching naked girls swim past. But he never made it. Now the boat sits low in the water, the hull coated with moss and barnacles, the moldy sails unraveled along the lowered mast. The portholes are coated with mold, and when I go on deck I can't even see into the cabin. But Griff doesn't want me to see if everything's okay inside. He just wants me to see that it's still afloat.

I glance up, following the bow of Griff's boat out across the water. Just around the point is the bay and beyond the bay the Golden Gate Bridge, and beyond the bridge nothing but ocean. Griff could have just sailed away, even if it was not to the South Seas, only to a little village down the coast of Baja, someplace to start fresh, someplace where they didn't know him, someplace where he didn't know himself—a place without speed or booze, a place of calm beside the water. But he never left.

Now he rides a motorcycle to daily AA meetings. I gave him a job with one of my clients, but he cost me the business when employees arriving for work found Griff passed out naked on the CEO's sofa.

When I asked him why he did it, he laughed the crazy laugh all the Woolf men possess: a loud, cackling sound, as if the voice in the black box had stopped asking to be let out and started laughing at being trapped instead. I know I still have that laugh. I just try not to let it out too often.

I head back to my car. Night is coming, and multi-million dollar homes are lighting up on Belvedere. Across the bay another array of lights blazes up—the brightest spot in sight—like an enormous stadium open for a night game.

One more stop.

Twenty minutes later I park at the edge of the web of light. I can even see Paradise Cove, where I had been looking across to where I am now.

Getting out of the car, I walk closer to the gate, stopping to gaze up at the gun tower North Block, East Block, the roof over Death Row, and all the unseen places I know by heart. "Nine years of my life I spent inside that place," I think.

Maybe it's the wind off the bay that chills me. "Just one more look," I think, staring all the way across San Quentin.

The guard at the entrance tilts his head away from the light to get a better look at me. "What can I do for you?"

I glace up at the walls. "Nothing. I just wanted to see the prison." I walk back to get into my car and pause for a moment. The sky is clear and cloudless all the way to the horizon. Above me, stars glitter from the darkness. I stare at the brightest one I can find. Out of nowhere after all the years, lost lyrics return:

"Like a bolt out of the blue, fate steps in and sees you through.
When you wish upon a star, your dreams come true."
No more walls for me. Time to go home.

The End

978-0-595-41557-1
0-595-41557-1

Printed in the United States
70285LV00002B/301-348